I

A Novel

By

John Steinmetz

Diverged
First Edition

Copyright © 2023

ISBN: 979-8-218-16503-1

Published by

Contour Press
Chevy Chase, Maryland

www.ContourPress.com // (301) 587-4343

For Melanie.

My everything.

Two roads diverged in a wood, and I –
I took the one less traveled by,
And that made all the difference.

-- Robert Frost --

1 - BROTHERS

Let me tell you a story. It's a good story. Well, I think it's a good story but of course you can judge for yourself. There are plenty of people who would be able to tell it better than myself, but unfortunately for you, they aren't here, so you're stuck with me. I'll break a few literary rules along the way. I'm probably doing that right now. The way I look at it though, it's my story – my rules. Are you ready? OK then, let's get started.

I've known three people in my life. Alfred Forman, Mark Lorenzo, and Bruce Fitzpatrick. I've met thousands of acquaintances, hundreds of colleagues, dozens of family members, and a few too many enemies, but I haven't actually known any of them in the true sense of the word. With Alfred, Mark, and Bruce, it's been different. For as long as I can remember, I've known what they were thinking without them saying a word. I could see it in their faces. I could see it in the way they would move. I could see it in the words they were not saying, and in the way they would push through the turnstiles at subway stations. It's an innate connection with three other humans that I've never had with anyone else previously or since.

Oh... for the purpose of introduction, my name is John Schumacher. There are two John's you're going to have to keep up with when you are reading this. The first is John NARRATING the story from the perspective of an outsider looking in (that would be me in italics), and the second is John TELLING the story from the perspective of the story insider (also me, but not in italics). Clear as mud??

Am I being too chatty? Don't worry, I'll only interrupt when I feel I need to... or whenever I feel like it since I'm doing all the work here! Anyway, Nice to meet you, and back to it...

The four of us have... how can I say this... lived our entire lives in a parallel universe. We were all born within a couple of years of each other in the mid to late 1950's on Staten Island, and grew up as neighbors on

Davis Avenue, a working-class area of the city largely populated with policeman, fireman, and shopkeepers. We've known each other for as long as we've been able to piss standing up, and that's probably why our ethnicity never seemed important to us. My ancestors were from Germany, Mark's from Italy, Bruce's from Ireland, and Alfred's from Africa. I only mention this because outside of our little world, this might seem important or interesting. Not to us though. Through our lenses, we were all from Davis Avenue, and nothing else really mattered. None of us have any siblings. Very strange for the baby boomer generation. None of us went to college, nor were we in the military. We've all had a few marriage prospects over the course of our lives but none of us were ever able to bring one across the finish line. That led to none of us having children. We all have blue collar jobs. We all attended P.S. 45 grammar school, Prall Junior High, and Curtis High School. I know these parallels seem unlikely, but that's exactly my point. Rarity often breeds value.

Allow me to pause the story here for a moment. I just thought of this and I think it may help you to better understand just how cemented this little group is, both in terms of history as well as group culture. It will be told by the "other" John, but he would have skipped right over it if it wasn't for me. It's not that he's lazy, but he does have a tendency to be forgetful.

As children, we established our own societal rules pertaining to various inevitable events. Three of these rules come to mind immediately. The first rule was known as "CHIPS". If someone in our group accidently broke something that belonged to one of the others, the "breaker" and the "breakee" would rush to yell out either CHIPS (the breakee) or NO CHIPS (the breaker). The first one to call out would win, and that would decide if financial or replacement restitution would be required or not. The second rule was "SLAPS". This rule is similar to CHIPS in that speed is the key to winning or losing. When one of us would become the unfortunate recipient of a fresh haircut, it was incumbent on that person to defend himself by yelling NO SLAPS before one of the others yelled SLAPS. If the haircut recipient was too slow, he had to let the winner slap him on the back of his neck at full strength to inaugurate the new haircut. The primary difference between CHIPS and SLAPS is that with the former, you had to defend yourself against each group member you encountered. This often led to an extremely red neck if you didn't remain alert for at least two days. After that, the haircut was no longer considered "new" and the SLAPS rule expired. The third rule was called "SKIPS". This rule referred to sneakers that were anything other than Converse (Chuck Taylors) or Pro-Keds. These were the only acceptable shoes in our neighborhood. If you had a mother who, as in my case, refused to pay the ten dollars for Converse, stating that the knock-off sneakers she picked up for half the price were just as good, you would have to pay the difference, with pain being the local currency. Speed and vigilance would again rule the day, so it all came down to who first yelled SKIPS, or NO SKIPS. If the humiliated party was too slow, the other would be allowed to stamp one time on the offender's feet as hard as he could. Of course, as with the other rules, if the offender was quick enough with his defensive shout, the pain was averted. These three rules were set in stone. No exceptions. When there was a rare disagreement about who made their verbal claim first, the others in the group would be the adjudicators. The process worked well and was fair to all.

I hope that helps your understanding of the group dynamic a little better. I thought it might be interesting to see how even the smallest and youngest of groups develop rules to live by within their clan. When you get toward the end of the story, you will better understand its importance. But then again, I never claimed to be Hemingway. I'm pretty sure he would have cut me out of the story completely.

OK, I hear you... I'll try not to interrupt as often from this point forward. The operative word here is "TRY."

Mark is a co-owner, as well as occasional cook, at a local pizza joint at the end of our street. I guess you could say he's the hothead of the group. He once told me that Italians tend to be blunt, and this is often mistaken for rudeness. While that particular assessment is bullshit, it certainly is true that Mark will say exactly the first thing that pops into his head, and won't give a damn if it pisses off everyone who might be in earshot of the comment. He also happens to be the smallest of the four of us. This is important because when his impetuousness leads him to say the wrong thing to the wrong person, it falls on the rest of us to step in. Frankly, I'm getting too old for bar fights.

By contrast, Alfred is the calmest of the four of us, which is good because he's also the biggest lug that I know. His biceps are the size of my thighs. Of course, the rest of us would never admit to his face that his size is somehow intimidating to us. Quite the opposite. We often will look for opportunities to tell him to watch himself or he'll suffer the consequences. This, of course, is just trash talk that is designed to keep his ego in check. We all know deep down that if he ever actually decided to hit us, we would drop like a sack of flour. Al has a great sense of humor though, and I'd be a wealthy man if I had a dime for every hour the two of us sat on a porch making each other laugh until we cried.

Have you ever seen a giant cry? Well, it's weird; I can tell you that much.

So, I guess I would say Alfred is the clown of the group. He sells cars at a local dealership, a good job for someone who is immediately liked by almost everyone he meets, and he also makes pretty good money working on the side as a damn good freelance mechanic.

Are you wondering if I get the "friend discount"? Not just NO but HELL NO! Look reader... I'm going to interrupt any time I want. That much should be clear to you by now. Live with it.

Bruce is the brains of our quartet. If he could have found a way to go to college, he would have made a great lawyer or CEO of some company. Unfortunately, his parents didn't have the means to send him, and he started working shortly after high school to help them out financially. He works at the Staten Island Advance newspaper maintaining the presses and generally telling everyone else who works there how they should do their jobs. He can be annoying when he does that but he's also full of interesting, though mostly useless facts. He takes on the role of tour guide whenever we take the ferry into Manhattan, pointing out various lesser-known points of interest such as Alexander Hamilton's grave at Trinity Church, and Fraunces Tavern where George Washington gave his farewell speech to the troops. I should say for clarity's sake that Bruce is in no way pretentious. He just enjoys and is well versed in historic trivia, and when he shares that with others, he does so as an expression of friendship. It's like he's giving us a gift, and we have learned to accept it as such.

As for me, I work for the Con Edison electric company. I was lucky. One of my cousins worked there, and got me an entry-level job to get my foot in the door. Over the years I've been able to work my way up to become a lineman. I'm not exactly sure what my role is in the group. Alfred once laughingly proclaimed I was voted by the others as "Most Likely to Become a Priest." But if I had to put a label on myself, I would say I'm the peacemaker of the group. When the others start fighting, as they inevitably do, it's up to me to remind them what morons they are, which is usually enough to get them to forget about whatever they were fighting about while making counter-accusations toward me that typically focus on my manhood or some aspect of my hygiene. I've become pretty good at my role, and most of these arguments end up in laughter. Friends fight, but if they're true friends they get over it quickly.

Listen up Ladies … You may not realize this, but it's normal for guys to get into verbal or sometimes physical altercations with their friends. Don't worry. It's not a big deal. Think of it as a kind of bonding ritual. Guys only start to worry when the harassment stops. OK, keep reading.

Perhaps the oddest parallel between us is that none of us ever moved from Davis Avenue. As kids, the boundary surrounding Davis Avenue between Forrest and Harvest avenues belonged to us. It was our territory, and anyone else who ventured in were either suspicious outliers or simply irrelevant passersby. Now that we're all in our sixties, that boundary remains intact in our collective hearts. The four of us have weathered all storms, and I'm comfortable saying our friendship is shatterproof. Our connection to Davis Avenue is equally invulnerable.

✳

One winter evening, I don't remember the exact year but it was sometime while we were still in our thirties, Mark's parents died prematurely. It was an accident involving a carbon monoxide leak from an old furnace that should have been replaced years prior. Mark wasn't home at the time. He was working a late shift at the restaurant, and stopped for a couple of beers afterwards. By the time he got home, it was all over. He found his father dead on a couch in front of the TV, and his mother had died in her bed. After opening all the windows in the house that weren't permanently stuck in place, Mark called me. I was still awake when he called, so I was standing beside him within minutes. I checked both parents for a heartbeat and breathing, finding neither. I asked Mark if he called the police yet, and his blank stare was as clear a response as I needed. I made the call. Both the fire department and the police arrived within minutes, immediately followed by the arrival of Alfred and Bruce who heard the commotion and simultaneously burst through Mark's door, nearly knocking over a police officer who was standing just inside the threshold. The three of us surrounded Mark in the same way a herd of elephants would surround one of their own in danger. He was in shock, and we were there to make sure nothing else would hurt him that night. He would have done the same for any of us.

The memories and the wounds from that terrible night eventually yielded to the push and persistence of life. Mark inherited his parent's 60-plus year-old Craftsman style home. In time, Alfred, Bruce, and I walked similar journeys. As we lost our parents, we too inherited the homes we had grown up in. The cycle was complete. The last names on the mail delivered to our four houses would be maintained for at least one more generation. This continuity further cemented our claims to Davis Avenue aristocracy.

The years passed. I never really cared for the term "life marches on", but it does. With each passing day, the four of us fell into the cadence of our lives. We woke up, we would go to work, and we would come home only to work on whatever home repair was needed. This in itself was a full-time job for our 1920's vintage homes. To break this cycle, we would get together whenever we could for drinks, cigars, or maybe a marathon round of Monopoly. The game had become something of a tradition on our street, especially on those long hot summer weekends. We would gather on one of the four front porches with great anticipation. As with many Monopoly aficionados, we had our own modified house-rules that suited our needs, and the games were necessarily, and exquisitely ruthless. The yelling, and the laughing inevitably drew onlookers from around the neighborhood. They didn't seem to have any interest in joining the games but they clearly enjoyed sharing our beer while observing grown men engage in mostly bloodless battles of real estate domination. The games were cathartic, and they were exactly what we needed.

I'm constantly reminded by my body as well as my mirror that I'm no longer a kid. Hell, I can't even pretend to be a man in his prime anymore. The 21st Century is in its third decade, and I still think of it as an infant. My age has arrived hand-in-hand with personal introspection. At the risk of falling into some philosophical dribble, let me say that as I have aged, I find myself thinking less about how I landed in this place, and more about why I landed in this place. I've come to a couple of conclusions on the subject. For instance, I no longer ponder my fate. My fate is the same as everyone's. I'm eventually going to die. I've lived a lot of years, and I haven't met anyone who has done otherwise, so I'm pretty damn comfortable with this conclusion. My destiny, on the other hand, is something entirely different. Destiny precedes fate; sometimes by years and sometimes by seconds. At one time I was worried I wouldn't recognize my destiny when it approached. Worse yet, I wondered if I had already fulfilled my destiny without even realizing it. I have been freed of these fears. I have come to believe that my destiny is, and always has been, inexorably bonded to those of three friends. This bonded destiny will play out in its own way, and in its own time.

Are you still with us reader? We didn't mean to wade into the deep end of the pool. If the other John goes there again, I'll say something to him. Hang in there!

2 - A PLANTED SEED

My first inkling that my friends and I needed something different in our lives, something to add a spark to our daily routine, was a few days before we would be making our weekly pilgrimage to O'Leary's Pub. I was on the bus coming back from a doctor's appointment in St. George, when I overheard a conversation between two kids. They were probably in their late twenties or early thirties but I use the word "kids" because I was certain they would have no idea that Joe Pepitone was the first baseman and outfielder for the Yankees in the sixties. So yeah… kids. They were talking about trips they had made recently; one to somewhere in Europe and the other to Hawaii. One particular comment gave me pause.

"My parents have never been anywhere except here. I intend to explore as much of this world as I can before I'm buried. We only get one shot at life, and I sure don't want to waste it. There's just too much to experience out there to let it pass unseen."

Now typically I wouldn't give two cents for what some punks on a bus thought about anything, but for some reason this comment had an impact on me. I began to make a mental list, a very short list indeed, of my journeys beyond the city limits. As a child I had been to the Finger Lakes region in upstate New York and to Niagara Falls during a family vacation. Another year, our family went to Montreal to visit Expo '67. We also had relatives who lived on a farm in south Jersey where we would make occasional visits. Other than that, my life has been pretty much confined to the five New York boroughs. This really isn't as uncommon for New Yorkers in my age group as you may think. I remember as a teenager watching tourists on the Staten Island Ferry taking pictures of the Statue of Liberty and the downtown skyline, and feeling sorry for them. I couldn't imagine how disappointed they must have felt having to live somewhere else in the country. This feeling, that I was already in the best place in the world, justified sticking close to home. Now I began to wonder if it was me, rather than those tourists on the ferry, who was missing out. The more I thought about it, the more determined I became to find out. I also knew I had three others I needed to convince.

O'Leary's Pub sits in a row of attached businesses on Forrest Avenue close to where it intersects with Bement Avenue. It's a long and narrow Pub with a polished dark wood bar on one wall that accommodates about a dozen customers, and a half dozen small round tables that line the opposite wall. It has a tile floor and a tin-lined ceiling, both original to the early twentieth century structure. It's one of those small businesses in New York that has been there longer than we've been alive, and was previously frequented by our fathers and grandfathers. In the sixties and seventies there was nothing to eat there unless you could stomach the stale mixed nuts or the vat of pickled eggs that tempted the braver patrons to "Eat me if you dare!" These were the years when it was not uncommon for a hat to be passed around to support the Irish Republican Army during "The Troubles." Thankfully those times have past, and the only troubles we experience now are those generated within our own group and with far milder consequences.

Aside from what can be seen and touched, there is also something ethereal about the pub. It's hard to put my finger on what I mean, but it's almost as if the pub itself is glad when I'm there. The lighting is kept very low and it generally takes a minute for my eyes to fully adjust, especially on those rare occasions when I arrive before sundown. Once they adjust, I feel like I've entered a harbor that has been providing temporary refuge from the storms of exhaustion and perturbation for nearly a century. I'm greeted and hugged by ghosts. It's a place where glasses are raised to toast friends, and memories of friends long gone.

The current proprietor is Sean Gallagher. My friends and I first met Sean years ago at Curtis High School, and even back then he was known as someone whose bark was much worse than his bite. We actually like him, but we go out of our way to make sure he doesn't know that. We've been gathering there each Friday evening for years, and we have an unspoken rule that we don't make phone calls or send texts to let the others know we'll be there. It's assumed we'll be there unless one of us calls to say he can't make it because of the amputation of a limb or something of equal or worse severity. When we were much younger, these weekly events would almost always end up with a fairly high level of shared intoxication, but since we all walked there, we didn't kill anyone while attempting to drive home. With a lot more age, and a tiny bit more maturity, we now spend less time drinking and more time talking. This is a fact that hasn't gone unnoticed by Sean who never seems to tire of referring to us as the four vagrants.

*

I arrived at the pub first around 7:30pm. Without asking, Sean brought a pitcher of beer, and four glasses to the table. He knew our routine as well as we did. Alfred and Mark walked in together shortly after that. Mark made a beeline for Sean who was standing at the bar as Alfred sat down at the table. Al looked tired as he plopped down. I spoke first.

"What's going on man? Looks like you had a rough day."

"Yeah… you know. Same shit but I'll survive. I'm glad we've got the weekend to look forward to. How about you?"

"Yeah, pretty much the same. Help yourself to a beer."

About that time, Mark started moving in our direction but not until he whispered something to Sean that was obviously intended to provoke a response. This provocation was ignored with nothing more than a glare from Sean. Mark shot us a grin and a wink when he joined us.

"How's it going John? Where's Bruce?"

"Pretty good Mark. I don't have the Bruce watch today but he'll get here before 8:00. He told me yesterday he was breaking in some new kid at work, so I suspect that's slowing him down."

Mark nodded and poured himself a beer. He flicked his head in Sean's direction.

"We may need to put that poor bastard down soon. It doesn't seem to matter what I say to him anymore, I can't seem to get a rise out of him."

Alfred leaned forward on the table to significantly

close the distance between himself and Mark. They were nearly nose-to-nose when Al spoke.

"You know, someday you're going to say something to him that puts him over the edge. I don't really care if he shoots you, but if I have to find another place to hang out on Friday nights, I'm not gonna be happy."

Mark looked incredulously at Alfred and without a pause, responded.

"Shoot me? That's a laugh! Hitting me with his purse is more likely."

We were all still laughing at this when Bruce walked in. He said something in Gaelic to Sean who acknowledged in kind while making a quick glance over to our table.

More Gaelic followed and although I obviously couldn't understand a word of it, I correctly assumed that Mark was the subject. Bruce looked over to us for a second, and then dropped his head. I could see by his face that he was frustrated or disappointed or both. I just wasn't sure why. Bruce nodded to Sean and walked over to us. He put one hand on Mark's shoulder without any greetings.

"What did you say to him this time?"

"Nothing bad! I just asked him about his mother."

"And what exactly did you ask him about his mother?" Bruce asked.

"I asked if she was still walking the streets."

Then with his signature shit-eating grin, Mark added, "Damn, you'd think Sean would be happy that someone besides himself, and one of his mom's johns, would be kind enough to think about her."

It was one of those moments when you knew you shouldn't laugh. Mark was relentless with Sean, not because he didn't like him, but because Sean was an easy target. When a child acts like this, you would never say or do anything to encourage further bad behavior. But it was no use. All four of us immediately broke out into hysterical laughter.

*

Our Friday evening pub gatherings typically take on an informal, but fairly consistent agenda. First, we exchange some good-natured ribbings, such as denigrating someone's mother, girlfriend, or spiritual leader. Next, we would move on to argue over whatever sport season was in play. We would vigorously debate which New York teams were best. The options were Yankees or Mets during baseball, Giants or Jets during football, Knicks or Nets during basketball, and Rangers or Islanders during hockey. The way it has always broken out within our group is Yankees-Giants-Knicks-Rangers preferred by Mark and myself. In uniform opposition are Alfred and Bruce's misguided preferences for the Mets-Jets-Nets-Islanders. The only thing we could all agree on was that the Red Sox-Patriots-Celtics-Bruins sucked. The rest of the agenda was filled in by whatever the topic-of-the-day may be that particular week. When we ran out of sports steam, it was my opportunity to throw out the recommendation I'd been concocting for a couple of days.

"Listen guys, I've got something I want to propose to all of you."

This got their attention, and the table fell uncharacteristically silent.

"I think we need a change of scenery and I'm not talking about a different Pub. Personally, I've only ventured from the city a few times, and that was years ago. I know this is true for the rest of you as well, so I'd like to suggest we take a road trip."

Nothing but silence. I interpreted this as… "keep talking asshole" … so I did.

"Look at it like this. I've got leave built up at Con Ed, and Bruce, you told me recently that you also have excess leave waiting to be used. Mark, I know you run the restaurant, but I'm pretty sure Bennie is capable to keep things running if you were to decide to take a vacation. Last time I checked, as your partner, he's more than capable.

I didn't wait for a response. I wasn't finished making my case.

"Al, I know you work primarily on commission at the dealership, and this would stop if you're not there to sell cars. The same would be true of your side job as a mechanic; if you're not working on cars, you won't get paid. So, you'll have to decide if this is something you can work out financially."

Alfred interjected before I could continue. He abruptly slid his chair back a bit and slapped one of his large hands on the table. The rest of us grabbed our beers to steady them.

"I'm in!" he yelled.

This took me off guard, and I knew I had to slow down the rush to judgment if I had any hope of getting the others to agree. I responded before anyone else could.

"Hold on Al! I appreciate your enthusiasm but you need to hear the rest of this before you decide. I'm talking about a significant road trip."

I think Alfred's quick response shook the others a bit, and both started to weigh in before I could elaborate further. I was hit with rapid fire questions from Mark and Bruce, and I'm not even sure which question came from which mouth.

"Where do you want to go?"

"How long is this trip?"

"Fly, drive, train?"

"How much will this cost us?"

This put me on my heels, and I was definitely having some trouble reading the room. Were the questions showing a level of excitement born of enthusiasm about the trip, or were the questions intended to show how much this scheme would involve, and maybe something we should avoid altogether? The table went quiet again, perhaps so my friends could reload. I took the opportunity to continue before they could say anything else.

"Listen guys, everyone please slow down. I'm open to your suggestions of course, but I was thinking about a two-week trip to Key West. I know money is an issue so hear me out. To save some money I think we should drive rather than fly, splitting the gas three ways. Whichever car we take, the owner doesn't pay for gas. I thought we could save additional money by getting two motel rooms at stops along the way, two of us per room. We would use less-expensive places like Motel 6 or Sleep Inn. If everyone can get the time off, I think we can do this on-the-cheap. Here's my one requirement. We either agree to do this as a group, or we don't do it at all. I wouldn't want to go if we don't all go."

Silence. At least it seemed like everyone was seriously considering the idea. Bruce spoke up.

"OK, since you brought it up, whose car do we take if we decide to do this? None of us can brag about having the greatest car in the world. I think mine is the newest but I've had some issues with it recently. Nothing big, but Key West is a long drive."

This was a good sign. By getting into the weeds, it meant that at a minimum, the plan wasn't being dismissed out-of-hand. I had already anticipated Bruce's question, knowing he was the ultimate pragmatist.

"I would suggest we rely on Alfred to make that call. He's the mechanic in the group. My initial thought would be to take Mark's Taurus, but that's only because it will comfortably accommodate four people and our luggage. But I'm not married to that. Al, what do you think?"

"I can give the car a good check, but for now I agree with the choice. It's a solid car with a dependable engine, and even though it has some years on it, the milage is still pretty low. Plus, if anything does go wrong, I would probably be able to fix it once I got whatever parts I needed. I may not be able to say the same if we choose one of the other three cars. In my opinion, Bruce's VW and John's old Volvo would be no-go's right out of the gate. My Corolla is a good car, but it's too small for the four of us."

Alfred paused for a second, but we all knew he had something else to say, so we waited for him to say it. It seemed like a long pause, but I'm sure it was much shorter than it felt. I wondered if he was pondering the costs, being the only one whose income was completely dependent on being at work.

"You're right, John, about my income coming to a pause if we make this trip. My commissions, and my side-job make up almost everything I bring in. I've had a good year though. Sales have been strong, and I've had more mechanical repair work than I've been able to keep up with. As I said before, I'm in."

Bruce jumped in right after Alfred. I was least worried about Bruce since I knew he had paid leave on the books. He didn't disappoint.

"Why not? I could definitely use some time away from work." He thought for a second as he reached for a quote. He chose one borrowed from JFK. "If not now, when?"

Ha! Bruce and his historic references. The guy cracks me up!

We all looked over to Mark. Because we were so close to my self-imposed requirement for unanimous consent, the anxiety level in me grew. This thing that I thought we so desperately needed all hinged on his response. I set it up for him.

"OK buddy, I guess it all comes down to you. You've been pretty quiet about this, so what's it going to be? Do you trust Bennie not to burn down the restaurant if you take this trip?"

In true Mark fashion, he didn't take any time at all to consider the question or to choose his words carefully.

"I'm less concerned about a fire at the restaurant than I am about being stuck in a car for days with a bunch of trash talking, junk eating, bad smelling, jack offs!" Smiles around the table.

His response didn't exactly point to which way he was leaning, so I should have remained quiet and waited. Should have... but didn't. I had a feeling in my gut that it was no time to show Mark any signs of weakness.

"Let me ask you something Mark. Do you think your ass ever gets jealous of the amount of shit that comes out of your mouth?"

The smiles turned to laughter around the table. Luckily, my gut didn't let me down, and it was Mark's laughter that nearly drowned out the rest of us.

"Well Hell's-Bells brother" Mark replied, "I guess we're going to Key West!"

3 - THE DETAILS

We divvied up responsibilities for the trip. Since it was my idea initially, I was assigned the job of planning out the schedule. It was up to me to propose where we would stop along the way, and how long we should stay at each location. Once I was done with that, I would turn it over to Bruce who would use my inputs to research which hotels we would stay at, keeping in mind, we all wanted to make the trip as inexpensive as possible without having to resort to fleabag hotels. Alfred would check out Mark's Taurus to make sure it was ready for the trip, and if not, to determine which of the other three cars would be best to use. Mark had the most difficult job of the four of us. He was responsible for staying out of trouble long enough for us to get to Key West and back. It was a tongue-in-cheek job assignment. Well, sort of. The truth is, we really couldn't think of anything else we needed to prepare, but he did offer to make a bunch of sandwiches to take along, and that sounded great to the rest of us.

While everyone was onboard with the idea of the trip, we all agreed that one final decision point was needed after the planning was completed, and everyone had a chance to review it.

The Devil is in the details.

We all agreed that we could be ready to travel within a few weeks, which would have us leaving sometime around mid-October. This was my starting point for laying out a travel plan. Our next gathering at O'Leary's would be dedicated to presenting the plan for everyone to review, and hopefully approve. I could sense a level of excitement between us that I hadn't felt in quite a while. Something new. Something different. An adventure!

The next morning (Saturday), I wasted no time getting started with my part of the planning. I was feeling a newfound energy that was driving me to action. I also knew Bruce needed my inputs before he could start his part of the plan. There was no time to waste. I jumped out of bed, made myself a strong cup of coffee, and flipped opened my laptop. Breakfast would have to wait. I opened Google Maps to scout out potential stops based on distance, time of departures, and arrivals. I opened up a Google search session to make sure that wherever we stopped, it would have a good selection of hotels and places to eat. This would make Bruce's job a little bit easier.

I started by doing a search for potential upcoming activities in Key West during the timeframe I was considering. I thought that if any special events would be falling within our travel window, we may wish to adjust our plans to either make sure we got there in time to participate, or to avoid the impacted dates completely. I was glad I checked. Google revealed something called Fantasy Fest in Key West, October 21st through October 30th. It was described as:

> *Fantasy Fest is a festival of thousands of fun-loving party people who descend on Key West every October for an adults-only extravaganza. Party people dressed in wild costumes mingle in the lively streets while drinks flow freely to get everyone into the spirit.*

Oh yeah, we DEFINITELY needed to be there for that! So, I had my first marker – arrive in Key West on October 19th. This would give us a little over a day to get our bearings before the start of Fantasy Fest.

I just heard one of you out there wondering aloud if Fantasy Fest is a real thing in Key West. Yup, it sure

is. Check it out!

I knew our first day on the road would be our shortest leg of the journey since I was thinking we wouldn't leave until after work. I decided that based on the targeted arrival date to Key West, we would leave Staten Island on Friday afternoon, October 14th. My primary goal for that part of the trip was to just get us out of the worst traffic areas. I thought somewhere south of Philadelphia would be reasonable. I opened Google Maps to see if I could identify a good candidate.

It seemed to me that one of the Delaware beach towns would be a good option for our first stop. Somewhere around the Lewes, Rehoboth, or Dewey beaches looked good since they were all very close to one another, and they were less than four hours from Staten Island. One thing I know about beach towns is they usually have plenty of hotels and restaurants. The other benefit that I picked up from Google Maps is that if we go that way, we could avoid having to drive through Baltimore and Washington D.C. the following day. I heard from a lot of people over the years that driving through Washington can be a disaster. I'm not sure why that's the case since D.C. isn't a huge city, but I figured better safe than sorry. The next day, we could drive south along the Delmarva Peninsula, crossing into the Norfolk, Virginia area via the Chesapeake Bay

Bridge Tunnel. From there we could make our way back to Interstate 95.

Assuming we left Staten Island by 4:30pm – I thought we could all leave work a bit early that day – we would get to our stop in Delaware in time for a late dinner followed by some drinks at a local bar. The next morning, October 15th, we could do a quick drive-through of the town and local sights, and then sometime before noon continue heading south toward our second stop in Lumberton, North Carolina.

This second leg to Lumberton would be about nine hours, plus a couple of hours for whatever stops we make along the way. I particularly had my sights set on a large cigar outlet in Selma, North Carolina. I didn't think I would get a fight on that one from my companions. Other than that, I didn't see much else to do along I-95 in North Carolina, but I would leave that to my co-travelers.

Our third leg of the trip would land us in Daytona Beach, arriving late in the afternoon of October 16th. This drive should only be about seven hours and even though we could easily push further south with four drivers, I thought stopping to see Daytona Beach was something we should do. It seemed to have a lot to offer, including the boardwalk at the beach, and a stop at the Daytona Speedway. I don't pretend to be a huge NASCAR fan, but for those who are, the Speedway is one of the iconic locations of the sport. You know what they say… "When in Rome…"

I also had another idea about something to do during our Daytona stop. I plan to keep this part of the trip secret until the actual day we are there. More on that later.

Our fourth leg would bring us to Miami. We certainly can't go to Florida without seeing some of Miami. It's about four hours from Daytona. We would arrive early in the afternoon on 18 October. It's good that we will get there fairly early in the day since we probably will need the extra time to see everything. If Mark can make it through one night without pasta, I'd love to visit a good Cuban restaurant before we leave Miami.

Our fifth and final leg of the journey would finally bring us to Key West on October 19th. The drive from Miami will be about four hours, getting us there plenty early to check in to wherever we decide to stay and to rest up for the start of Fantasy Fest!

I felt like Eisenhower couldn't have come up with a better plan for our Staten Island squad to storm the Key West beaches. I went over it a few times, and each time I did, I liked it a little more. I only hoped my companions would feel the same way. I intentionally left our return date from Key West open but I figured we could potentially stay for as long as ten days. We would decide that on the fly. My part was done. I printed out all of the details and brought it over to Bruce so he could take it from there. If anyone could take my travel schedule, and add inexpensive and decent lodging information, it was him. Bruce has always been great at getting good value for his money. OK… he's a bit of a cheapskate… but that's what makes him perfect for this part of the plan. Bruce committed to returning his portion of the plan back to me before Friday. I talked with Alfred who told me he already had arranged for Mark to bring his car over to the house so he could give it the once-over. Everything was set for a Friday review at O'Leary's followed by the "Go/No-Go" decision. I'm starting to feel what it must be like for an astronaut sitting on the launchpad.

4 - GO/NO-GO

When I woke up Friday morning, I hopped out of bed like I was a kid again. I still had to get through the work day but I knew that O'Leary's would be waiting for me on the other side. I was invigorated, excited, and completely frazzled. I fried up a couple of eggs and heated up some leftover sirloin steak that I had in the fridge. The coffee was already waiting for me thanks to the miracle of Mr. Coffee's timer. I sat down to watch the news with my breakfast, hoping the world was still there. It was. So far, so good.

Before leaving for work, I broke our unspoken rule. In a moment of weakness and stupidity, I sent a text to the guys asking if they all planned to be at O'Leary's that night. I was made to pay for that breech of etiquette. What was I thinking? Within seconds, the responses rolled in.

Mark swung first with his not-so-subtle brand of sarcasm.

"No. I NEVER go to O'Leary's on Friday nights …

Dickhead!"

Alfred then took his turn.

"Lay off him Mark. You know his dementia is getting the best of him."

Bruce was the most succinct.

"Moron."

I couldn't argue with any of that. I needed to get a grip! I responded with a simple poop emoji and finished getting ready for work. My job involves working around high-power lines and a lack of focus can be fatal. So, when I got there, I took a deep breath and put everything else, especially Key West, out of my head. One step at a time.

I think I was at work for about a week that day. Eventually, 5pm struck and I was thankful for a routine day, devoid of anything critical that would have delayed me. That wouldn't have been unusual. On the way home I got off the bus, one stop early, to run into a convenience store to pick up four cigars. I was planning to pass them out following a final approval of the travel plan. I know… it was a jinx risk to make such a presumption … but I decided to stay positive, and hope for the best. The store was named Syd's. It was named after a guy who owned the place back in the 60's and early 70's named Sydney Kroll. As kids growing up in the neighborhood, we found Syd to be a real hard-nose. I'm not sure how such a miserable person was able to run a successful business dealing with people for so many years, but he somehow figured out how to do both. It was an attractive establishment for us kids, since it stocked candy and comic books. It also had a soda fountain with a half dozen counter stools where we could buy chocolate egg cream sodas or root beer floats whenever we were able to hustle up the required forty-five cents. But... dealing with Syd was rough. He didn't like it when we would take a comic book out of the rack for more than a few seconds. He would never miss an opportunity to reveal his displeasure.

"Hey boy, this isn't a library. If you want to read that comic, then you need to buy it. If not, put it back, and feel free to leave!"

He also didn't like it if we hovered for too long around the large selection of candy displayed just inside the store entrance. I'm sure he was convinced we were stealing some candy when he had his back turned. Now to be honest, we did help ourselves to a sample from time to time, but he didn't know that for sure, and we thought he was an ass for accusing us without proper evidence. He later added a glass sliding door to the case. It wasn't locked, but the sliding door made enough noise when opened to get his attention, thus reducing our five fingered discount opportunities. Syd died many years ago but the subsequent owners kept the name of the place since everyone in the neighborhood knew it as such, and it was cheaper to not change the signage out front.

When I arrived, I went directly to the cigar case, which replaced the candy case with the noisy glass door. Funny how the store seemed to know how my vices were evolving over the years. Anyway, I wanted quality cigars, so I picked out four Cohiba's. Under normal conditions, buying such an expensive brand of cigar would have been out of the question, but I was still in the "stay positive" frame of mind, and splurged for this one evening. Oh, in case you're wondering, yes – I did actually pay for the cigars. My days of stealing things from Syd's are long past. From there I walked home, and cooked up one of my favorite meals… a thick hamburger made with half beef and half pork. I didn't use a bun, instead opting for just the burger topped with cheddar cheese and jalapeno peppers with a whole pickle on the side. I boiled some frozen corn to go with this masterpiece. Completely nourished, I was ready for the big event.

Are you starting to get excited reader? Yeah, I think I can feel it. Or maybe you're just hungry. Go grab a snack and come back. GO! …

… Feeling better now? Blood sugar back where it needs to be? Good. Now, where was I? Oh yeah. So…

*

When I got to O'Leary's, I saw that Alfred had already arrived, and based on the level of beer in the pitcher, I guessed he was working on his second glass.

"Big Al... what's going on dude?"

He looked up from his glass and nodded. He pointed to a chair and said "Take a load off."

"I'm surprised to see you beat me here. That almost never happens."

"True, but I had a feeling you would be particularly anxious to get things started tonight. I would have texted you to let you know I'd be here early, but that would have required me to wear a dress."

This was, of course, a continued jab at my earlier texting faux pas to the group. I couldn't help but smile.

"Are you done?"

"Not by a longshot! But I do have some good news for you. I looked over Mark's Taurus and it will be fine for the trip. I changed the oil, checked all the fluids, and the tires are in good shape. I also checked the plugs. They were fine. Nothing is ever 100 percent but I'm comfortable taking it to Florida."

I wasn't surprised by this but it was a welcomed first check-mark on our travel list and I was certainly grateful for that.

"Fantastic Al! I really appreciate you doing that."

"No problem. It was easy. You and Bruce had the harder jobs. How did that go?"

Alfred's initial enthusiasm had obviously not waned.

"Good, but let's wait until Mark and Bruce get here before discussing it."

"Yep. They should be here any minute."

Alfred was right. Mark walked in within ten minutes and Bruce soon followed. We all greeted one another (thankfully with no additional text related comments from Mark or Bruce) and we got right down to business.

I started by mentioning that Al gave the Taurus a thumbs up for the trip. I then stepped through the scheduled stops, adding in the hotel information that Bruce provided. He did his typically thorough analysis, recommending hotels at each stop that were perfect for us. The places he chose were inexpensive yet decent places that received good reviews from previous guests. They included the Rehoboth Sleep Inn, a pair of Motel 6's in Lumberton and Daytona, and the Beach Park Hotel in Miami. Once in Key West, Bruce planned our stay at a renovated 1960's style motel called the Orchid Key Inn. This motel offered a fantastic location, right on Duval Street, and like the other stops along the way, the price was within our budget.

Bruce jumped in after I mentioned the hotels.

"Based on the prices I found online, and assuming we get two rooms each night splitting the costs evenly, I believe we'll be able to spend two weeks on the road for a cost of a little over one thousand dollars total for each."

Everyone seemed to be happy with that, and probably a little relieved. Bruce continued.

"Of course, that doesn't include meals, although the motels include breakfast each morning with the exception of the one in Key West. It also doesn't include gas, bar bills, and whatever other incidental costs we accumulate, but the hotel costs go a long way toward keeping our costs down. Luckily, we're travelling during off-season."

Alfred was nodding his head in agreement, and Mark spoke up.

"That all sounds good Bruce. I was frankly worried about the costs given what other people in the restaurant were telling me about Key West. But I gotta tell you man, if we can even get close to your estimate, I'll be happy."

Bruce then gave us a bit more detail about our stay in Key West.

"Well, just for the sake of total transparency, the place in Key West isn't exactly luxury accommodations. It's an older motel that was renovated. The rooms are small, but I really think it will be good for us since the prices are reasonable and the location is great, right on Duval Street. Each of you should check it out online but I think you'll be happy with it."

Alfred laughed and threw in his two-cents.

"Listen dude, it sounds great for the price. I don't think any of us need anything fancy, and it sounds like this place offers everything we'll need. I really like that we're on that street you mentioned... What was the name again?"

Bruce interjected.

"Duval Street."

"Yeah, OK, Duval Street. Anyway, you guys did a great job pulling this together so quickly. We can also save a lot of money if we can avoid paying out a bundle of cash in bail money. What do you think Mark?"

Mark snickered and gave Al the middle finger without responding aloud.

With that, it was time for the four of us to give our final "GO/NO-GO" vote. This time, the only fingers that went up were thumbs. It was a unanimous decision. The road trip, which had monopolized my thoughts for days, was actually going to happen! I was excited... and I was thankful... and I was nervous. I didn't ask the others what they were feeling, although I was curious. But I knew if the shoe were on the other foot, and they would have asked me how I felt, I would have downplayed my response with a simple "good." I knew they would have responded with a similarly ambiguous answer, so there was no point. I'm pretty sure that none of us will be invited onto "The View" to share our emotions.

It's a little weird to think it all started with a spark initiated by a couple of knuckleheads talking about their travels. I'm just glad I was on that bus and sat down within earshot of them. I read somewhere that Einstein once said "Coincidence is God's way of remaining anonymous." Who am I to argue with Einstein?

We left the bar early that night. There were some excellent cigars calling our names.

5 - DAY ONE

October 14th

We all agreed to leave work early on the 14th so we could target a 5pm departure from Staten Island. We would meet up at Mark's house with luggage in-hand, and attitudes checked at the door. I was hopeful for the former, and absolutely certain that the latter would collapse before the luggage was stowed in the trunk. I was correct on both counts, and the four of us couldn't have been happier about either. Speaking of the trunk, all four suitcases (actually it was one suitcase – Bruce's—and three duffle bags) fit nicely as I had hoped. We had a full tank of gas, sub sandwiches that Mark prepared, and the GPS was set for the Sleep Inn located between Lewes and Rehoboth beaches. Bruce made all of the hotel reservations so we were in that department for the entire trip. We were ready to go at 5:05pm with the GPS telling us to expect an 8:10pm arrival in Delaware. Mark took the first shift behind the wheel, saying he wouldn't need to be relieved since this first leg of our journey would be relatively short. No arguments from the rest of us.

Al spoke up as we drove over the Goethals Bridge linking Staten Island to New Jersey.

"Look over your shoulder boys. It's the last you'll be seeing of Staten Island for a couple of weeks!"

We all did. It was a strange feeling looking back at the fading island through the heavy mist and dark clouds that had settled over the area that day. It was exciting but there was something else. An uneasiness fell over me. I guess it was just a feeling that we were embarking on the trip of a lifetime. Something that we would probably only do once. I sensed nervous anticipation in the car, and it was telling when we responded with only silent nods.

As we headed south on the New Jersey Turnpike, we broke out the sandwiches Mark prepared for the first day of the trip. They were still warm thanks to the thermal bag he used. Now Mark has several talents. Some of those talents we can talk about, and some we can't. None, however, can compete with his ability to create culinary artwork. This includes sandwiches that he takes to the next level. For this trip, he made Pastrami Reuben sandwiches topped with Sauerkraut, melted Swiss cheese and Russian dressing, all stacked high on thick-cut Rye bread that he grilled crispy brown. I swallowed that first bite and a bit reluctantly shared with him my reverence.

"Good God almighty man, you nailed it! I can't ever remember eating a sandwich this good."

Alfred and Bruce still had mouthfuls, so they just made some grunting noises from the back seat while nodding their heads in agreement. Mark just smiled at first. I suspect he didn't quite know what to do with the compliment but he then held up half of his sandwich with one hand and responded "Buon Appetito!"

We hit some traffic coming out of the city... all those New Jersey commuters going home from work... but we continued to move along at a decent pace, just a bit below the speed limit. Once we got past Exit 7, the traffic started thinning out and Mark had us clipping along at about 75 MPH after that. When we reached the southern end of the turnpike, I noticed a sign for the Penns Grove exit. This reminded me of my childhood.

"Hey guys! This is where my family would exit when we would visit my aunt and uncle's farmhouse. This is where I would hang out with four crazy-ass cousins. They enjoyed calling me "city boy" while we played around the farm, mostly collecting ticks and poison ivy rashes. Their house was a couple of hundred feet off the road, and to me, the farm may as well have been another planet."

Alfred was already sleeping off his Reuben and only

stirred slightly when I called out. Mark and Bruce showed no interest in pretending to care at all about this piece of my family history. Bruce only responded with an eye roll and a guttural "Hmmm." Mark, at least put some effort into his input.

"Big Whoop! If this is one of the highlights of the trip Schumacher, I'm turning this car around right now!"

He paused for a second before resuming his tirade.

"Just watch me, you Kraut. I'll damn well do it!"

What they failed to realize, and what I decided not to share based on their crystal-clear contempt, was that we just passed the most southern point that I'd ever ventured in my life. I doubt Mark and Bruce ever even made it this far. Alfred, I knew, had some family in Richmond, Virginia that he visited with his parents as a child. Our current travel plan had us passing close to Richmond not long after entering Virginia, and I decided that if Alfred says anything, I would pretend to be asleep just for a little bit of pay-back.

Within minutes of this exchange, we crossed over the Delaware Memorial Bridge into Delaware. We passed some exit signs for Philadelphia, at which point we veered off of I-95 and onto Route 1. This would eventually take us the rest of the way to our first stop – the Lewes and Rehoboth beaches. Along the way, we passed Dover Air Force Base, and a NASCAR track called Dover Motor Speedway. We briefly considered stopping to get a closer look at the speedway but decided that since we would be going to the track at Daytona, we would push on.

Most of what we saw from that point forward was rural farmland and roadside vegetable stands. It was a scenic and relaxing drive, and very different from the first part of our journey. As we got closer to the beaches, we started seeing more and more shops of all varieties and housing communities began popping up on both sides of the road. Shortly after this, we passed a large sign in the median welcoming us to Delaware's beaches.

The sun had dropped below the horizon but still offered the last of its glow in the sky before giving way to the stars. The GPS, which had been mostly quiet since we entered Delaware was now actively leading us to the Rehoboth Sleep Inn. It guided us through a U-turn followed quickly by a right turn past a Ford dealership, and into the hotel parking lot. Mark made the unnecessary announcement.

"Here we are boys. Stop number one, brought to you safely by me. Tomorrow it's my turn to be useless."

I laughed. "Fair enough dude. I'll take the first shift tomorrow. Let's check-in and figure out where we want to go for dinner."

✳

The hotel was nice. It looked fairly new, or else they must have recently renovated the place. We decided to mix up the room sharing arrangements as we went along, but for this first night Alfred and Bruce had one room and I would bunk with Mark. The rooms were perfect. Two queen sized beds in each room with a big flat-screen TV, a mini-fridge, and a Keurig coffee maker. The hotel also offered a free breakfast in the morning, which we may or may not take advantage of. By 8:30pm, we were settled in our rooms and ready to venture out for a late dinner and some drinks. We hadn't had anything since we devoured Mark's excellent sandwiches, and even though that was only about three hours ago, we were all hungry.

I volunteered to drive and said I would moderate how much I would drink. We decided to head south on Coastal Highway, which is Route 1, and we would just drive until we saw someplace that looked good. We passed some outlets, some fast-food places, and a couple of breweries, but we really wanted to find someplace that looked a little "beachier."

What he really means, is a place that looked more rowdy and maybe even more likely to have some women out for a good time on Friday night.

We passed the cutoff for Rehoboth Beach but stuck

to the plan of staying on Route 1. We agreed that if we didn't find anything good by the time we hit Bethany Beach, we would turn around and drive into the town of Rehoboth. Just as we were entering the Dewey Beach city limits, however, we came upon a place called Starboard. I pulled into the adjacent side street and asked for opinions.

"What do you think guys? This place looks great to me. Look at all these people here... I'm thinking it must be good."

Bruce spoke up. "Yeah man. This place is perfect. Find a parking spot and let's get in there."

Mark and Alfred both enthusiastically agreed. We had to go around the block before finding a spot, but that just increased the anticipation. When we got to the entrance, it was clear this place was crazy. People everywhere... loud music... TVs filled with various sporting events. It was different from anything we had on Staten Island. The layout was strange. It was a cacophony of open-air rooms, each with separate bars and round tables where the crowds gathered. It was as if three or four bars crashed into each other to create a nighttime cathedral dedicated to high spirits.

We ordered a pitcher of beer for the table, but before they even sat down, Bruce and Al decided to walk around the place. Mark and I waited for the beer and the menus. I noticed an uneasiness in Mark. I got the sense that he was deep in thought but doing his best to not let it show. Still, his body language was giving him away. He squirmed in his seat, he was spinning the ring that he usually wore on his index finger, and I thought he was intentionally avoiding eye contact with me. I knew he wanted to say something, but I also knew to let him come to it on his own time. I waited.

The waitress dropped off our pitcher, and the menus, and I thanked her. Mark and I both admired the view as she walked off, after which Mark decided to reveal what was on his mind.

"Hey man, I need to talk to you before the other two come back to the table."

I leaned in a little since he was sitting opposite me.

"Sure, what's up?"

"I met someone. A girl... well... a woman."

He seemed nervous and this wasn't like him. Now I was getting nervous.

"Okay, so you met a woman. What about it?"

"Well, I uhhh... well I'm going to ask her to marry me."

"What? No way Mark! You're pulling my leg."

He didn't start laughing, or slap me on the shoulder, or anything to indicate this was indeed his intent. He just looked down at the table, silently thinking of how to respond. I didn't wait for him to figure it out.

"Holy Shit! You're serious! Spill it fast... I want to

know everything."

I could see the stiffness in his body begin to relax. I think he realized that the hardest part of this conversation was over. He broke the big news that he'd obviously been holding back for a while, and now he just had to fill in the blanks.

"Her name is Isabel. Her family is from Puerto Rico, but she was born in Queens and she now lives on Staten Island, off of Richmond Terrace, not far from Mariner's Harbor. She's three years younger than me and she works in Manhattan as a paralegal in some law office."

"I'm still in shock here, man. Where and when did you meet her and why haven't I heard about her before this?"

"I know. I know. I first met her about six-months ago on the ferry. It was during the rush hour and the boat was packed and she asked if she could sit down next to me. She's beautiful, so of course I said yes. We just chatted; you know? Not about anything special but it was just a real comfortable conversation. So, I took a chance and asked for her phone number and she gave it to me. I called her shortly after that and we've been seeing each other ever since."

I think my mouth must have still been open from the initial reveal. It was a lot to take in all at once.

"Six months? Why didn't you tell us about this before now? Or is it just me you didn't tell? Do Bruce and Alfred know?"

"No, man, you are the first to know. I kept it a secret because I figured it wouldn't last. She kept asking me if I was going to introduce her to my friends but I kept putting her off. I think deep down I figured I would eventually fuck it up, and she would dump me. But she's like a saint. She's different from any other woman I've ever met. I don't need to hide who I am around her. I think that's what I like best about her. I can't believe she likes me!"

"Wow! She sounds great... but marriage? I never thought I'd see the day when one of the four of us would finally strike gold. You're gonna need to give me a little time to absorb all of this. Don't get me wrong... I'm happy for you... but jeez man, this is a shocker! And by the way, I can easily believe she likes you."

"Thanks, man. And yeah, I know I dropped a bomb on you, but if you think you're shocked, just think how I feel. For now, this is just between the two of us. Not a word to Al or Bruce yet."

"Oh no Mark, you can't do that to me – or them. You have to tell them tonight. I don't think I can hide my surprised look from them for the rest of this trip!"

He snickered at that. He was thinking as he stared at the table for a minute.

"OK, I won't make you keep it from them for the whole trip. Just until we get to Key West. I think that would be the most appropriate place for me to tell them. I only told you now because if I didn't tell someone, I would have exploded. You promise to keep quiet until then?"

I exhaled. I really didn't want to wait that long but I didn't think I had much chance at negotiating better terms with him. He knew I wouldn't betray his secret.

"Alright. I'll shake on that."

I stood up and put out my hand. He stood to reciprocate. As he extended his hand, I pulled him in, putting my left arm around his shoulders and offering him my congratulations as we shook hands.

That's an officially sanctioned Guy-Code hug as long as it isn't held for too long, and an appropriate air-gap is maintained.

After returning to our chairs, the conversation turned uncomfortable. Neither of us knew how to transition from Mark's bombshell news to a more casual discussion that Bruce and Alfred would expect when they returned. The best we could manage was to rely on a bit of small talk mixed with sips of beer and bites of food. We both looked over our shoulders from time to time, hoping to spot one or both of them returning to the table. As if on cue, Bruce approached the table with a cocktail in his hand, although Alfred was nowhere in sight.

"What are you guys talking about?"

Exactly the question we didn't want to hear. With surprising ease, Mark took his swing at responding without actually responding. His quick wit has always impressed me.

"We were just deciding what to do with your body after I strangle you this evening."

I didn't wait for Bruce to respond. I followed up Mark's diversion with my own attempt to quickly changing the subject.

"Where's Al?"

"Don't know. We went over to the bar and he started talking to a pretty lady mixing the drinks. After I got my drink, I just started walking around and exploring. This place is wild!"

I asked him if he knew we had the beer waiting at the table as I nodded toward the drink in his hand.

"Yeah, I know. Don't play Alcohol Police with me, Schumacher. I was just itching for a Jameson on the rocks."

"Hey man, I don't care what you drink as long as you keep it all inside of you. If you get sick in Mark's car, I don't think Alfred and me combined will be able to stop Mark from pushing your face in it."

Mark agreed without saying a word. He simply raised his glass toward Bruce as if to be proposing a toast and gave him a wink. Bruce sat down next to Mark and put his arm around him.

"Mark, you know I would never get sick in your car. But I did just fart on you."

Mark pushed Bruce away.

"Get away from me you disgusting Mick!"

We were all laughing when Alfred made his way back to the table.

One thing you should know about Alfred. He's a pretty good-looking guy, and he never had any problem attracting girls in his younger years. I guess he still has some of that attraction, I'm not the best judge of that, but like most of us, he sometimes has trouble remembering his age. He also struggles like the rest of us in judging the age of the fairer sex. This is problematic, especially since it's considered rude to ask a woman her age. When Al got to the table, he sat down and poured himself a beer.

"Hey guys… check this out. I was over at the bar and this chick poured me a drink and started talking to me. She keeps calling me "Honey" and "Sweety" and she's all smiles. I just came over to let you guys know that she's coming on strong and you shouldn't wait for me. When you're ready to go, just go. I plan to be busy. I'll Uber back to the hotel or maybe she'll drive me back."

This was like a gift from the gods. It was exactly what I needed to forget about Mark's secret, at least for this one night. Bruce almost ruined it. He chuckled at Al's comments about the girl and started to say something. I don't know which kick under the table hit him first... the one from me or the one from Mark. In any case, he managed to stay quiet, offering only a wide-eyed look at Mark and myself. I spoke up before Bruce changed his mind.

"Al, do you know how old this woman is? From what I've seen, the ladies working here are averaging at least 30 years younger than any of us!"

Before Al could answer, Mark jumped in.

"Yeah, and if you're not back by the time we leave tomorrow, we will definitely leave you. You'll have to find your way to the closest Amtrak station and take a train down to either Daytona or Miami. Fair warning my friend... we're not waiting for you."

"Jesus... Chill out Mark! I'll be back before you guys leave tomorrow. I just can't pass this up. She's really cute and I can't help it if she prefers mature guys."

Mark and I both had our feet ready to strike Bruce again, but he had apparently learned his lesson and remained quiet. Mark and I quickly glanced at each other, managing only the slightest hint of smiles at the corner of our mouths.

"OK, brother" I said. "Have a great time and we'll see you when we see you."

Al put two fingers to his brow in a type of boy scout

salute and walked back toward the bar. He was barely out of earshot before Bruce slapped the table.

"What the hell's going on? Why the kicks? Don't you know that the whole Honey-thing and the Sweety-thing is just the way the women talk down here? Do I have to explain everything to you guys? And I'm pretty sure that tonight isn't the first time in history a person who works mostly for tips is nice to a customer."

After Bruce was done stating the obvious, I stepped in to open his eyes.

"No shit Sherlock! Yes, we know that's how they talk here. We heard it at the hotel and we heard it from the hostess when we came in."

I let that sink in for a second. I could tell from the confused expression on his face that he still wasn't getting it.

"The important thing here, and the part you're missing... is that Al doesn't know that."

Mark laughed and pointed in the direction of the bar.

"Yeah, and he'll be heading back here with his tail between his legs before we finish these beers."

It finally became clear to Bruce what we were up to. He sat there shaking his head in disappointment as he often does.

"Man! You guys are brutal. I will admit, though, I'm looking forward to seeing the look on his face when he drags his ass back here."

Mark and Bruce drank freely from the pitcher but I babied my mug, knowing I had to drive on unfamiliar roads. We ordered some bar food – jalapeño poppers, nachos, some loaded fries, and waited impatiently for Al's retreat back to the home front. It took even less time than we thought. We spotted him walking slowly back to the table with his head down, and his hands in his pockets. Oh yeah, this went well.

"Welcome back, buddy! How was your date?" I asked.

Then Mark expressed his mock concern.

"Yeah Al, was it fun? I'm surprised you're back so soon. Do you need to borrow some money to buy her some flowers or to take her dancing somewhere?"

"Oh, shut the hell up!" Al popped one of the jalapenos.

I didn't hear exactly what he said over all the laughter, but I'm pretty sure there was something about her boyfriend mixed in with some colorful expletives aimed more at us than at her. By the time he finished off the nachos though, he seemed to be pretty much over his heartbreak. Bruce ordered himself another Jameson, and a pitcher of beer for the table as we settled down into a more age-appropriate evening of eating, drinking, and people watching. It was a good time. We got back to the hotel around 2am, and went right to our rooms to hit the sack. We had another long day ahead of us, and we don't spring back from all-nighters like we used to. The first day of our road trip was complete. It was a great start.

6 - DAY TWO

October 15th

The next morning, we took advantage of the free breakfast, and it really wasn't too bad. Afterwards, we gathered in the lobby to check out and discuss what would be next.

The guys seemed perfectly content for me to propose the itinerary. I suggested that before leaving the area, we should drive into the town of Lewes and then head over to the Cape Henlopen State Park, which is adjacent to the town. There were no dissents, so we packed up the car and headed out. I continued behind the wheel since there was very little driving the previous night. Within minutes, we were on the main shopping street in Lewes. It's a real small town that runs along a canal. Beyond the canal, I'd guess about a mile away, is Lewes Beach, and the state park is just a couple of miles from there.

We didn't stop anywhere in town; we just drove around checking things out. I was impressed by the near pristine look of the town. All of the historical houses were beautifully maintained. The Victorian era homes that lined the canal were particularly impressive.

OK, let me just say this. Schumacher wouldn't know a Victorian era home from a mobile home! He says stuff like that all the time, and with such a confident tone that people believe him. It doesn't really impact this story, but he's a known liar, and sometimes he just aggravates the hell out of me! Deep breaths.

As we drove further down the road that runs along the canal, getting further away from the town, something caught my eye on the water. I pulled into the dirt and gravel parking lot adjacent to a park. Alfred spoke up.

"What are we doing? Why did you pull over?"

I said "Look out the front window! Does something look familiar to you guys?"

Not surprising to me, it was Bruce who picked up what I was alluding to.

"Well, I'll be damned. Will you take a look at that. It looks like a twin of the Ambrose Lightship at the South Street Seaport."

"Bingo!... Let's go check it out" I replied.

I parked the car and we got out. It was still a bit early and the temperature was only around 45-50 degrees, but we didn't care. The first thing I noticed was a small shack where you would get tickets for a tour, but they were locked up tight. Probably for the season. Again, we didn't care. We were all a bit mystified by this twin of the lightship that as kids we used to explore. This was well before the South Street Seaport in New York was redeveloped, and became a major tourist attraction very near the Manhattan side of the Brooklyn Bridge. At the time, it was a dingy set of piers with its fair share of rats of both the rodent and human variety. We would take the ferry across from Staten Island and walk under the FDR Drive to the seaport. Nobody was there to keep a bunch of kids off the rusting red hulk that had the name "Ambrose" painted on the side. The ship we were standing in front of here in Lewes was strikingly similar, the biggest difference being the name painted on its side... Overfalls. Bruce, our resident historian, and tour guide, gave us his assessment.

Well, of course he did! He just can't help himself! Don't get me wrong, he's a pretty damn smart guy, it's just that sometimes I wish he'd... oh never mind. I'm still a little grouchy from Schumacher's "Victorian Era" comment. Back to Bruce's assessment.

"It's not exactly like the Ambrose, but it's close. The two appear to be about the same size, but I think the Ambrose is an older ship. This one has two lights stacked one on top of the other on a single mast, but the

Ambrose has two lights that are mounted on separate masts."

Bruce never fails to amaze me when it comes to this type of thing. He has an eye for detail and the memory of an elephant. I never would have noticed that the lights were mounted differently on the two ships without having them side-by-side.

Mark decided to propose his first stupid idea a bit earlier than he normally would. Typically, he needs a few cups of coffee before his brain starts short-circuiting.

"Let's go onboard!"

Alfred had something to say about that... "Mark, did you happen to notice the locked gate across the gang plank with a big red sign that says CLOSED?"

"Yes, I did, but as I recall, the Ambrose also had a similar gate, and we went over it without a second thought."

My turn... "Well, this isn't 1968 in a broken-down area of New York City. There are people all around here and I'd be willing to bet the police aren't far away either. I'm not climbing over any gate."

Bruce added his two-cents for good measure. "Yeah, let's use our heads for once. It's not worth a fine or a night in jail for trespassing. Besides, it's probably very similar to the Ambrose below deck."

Mark raised the white-flag. "Fine! Wusses!"

We piled into the Taurus and headed back through

the town, and over a small bridge that spanned the canal. Lewes Beach would be our next stop, followed by Cape Henlopen State Park.

*

It was a short drive. Just before we got to the beach parking lot, we saw a Dairy Queen. We're all suckers for DQ's Blizzards, no matter what time of year it is. When we were kids, we had the same affection for the Carvel ice cream place a couple of blocks away on Forrest Avenue. We didn't have money, of course, but we would barter with the owner. We would sweep up all of the cigarette butts and other trash in the parking lot, and he would give us free ice cream. Win-win!! My favorite back then was Carvel's "CMP." which stood for chocolate, marshmallow, and peanuts. Those ingredients were piled on vanilla soft-serve ice cream. My current favorite is DQ's Reece's Peanut Butter Cup Blizzard.

So, yes, we stopped at Dairy Queen. Four Blizzards later, we were back in the car and drove the short distance to the beach parking lot. Honestly... not a lot to see. It was a nice beach, although a little small and of course there were very few people there this time of year. We didn't linger long and continued down the road a short way to the state park.

Just beyond Lewes Beach was the Ferry Terminal for the Lewes/Cape May Ferry. Had I thought about it, I think I would have changed our route to drive to Cape May on the southern tip of New Jersey so we could have taken the ferry across to Lewes. That would have been cool. The only ferry any of us had ever been on was the Staten Island Ferry. Maybe there will be a 'next-time,' and if so, that's what we'll do. Not far beyond the terminal, we came to the entrance of Cape Henlopen State Park. We paid a small fee and entered. We weren't looking for anything in particular, just checking it out so we could say we've been there. We passed some camp grounds and then came upon a tall stone tower. We stopped to read the sign erected in front of the structure. Apparently, these towers were erected during World War II to spot German U-boats that were operating in the waters off of the east coast. They are not open to the public, which is too bad since they would have provided a great view. We moved on and passed a WWII vintage Army base named Fort Miles, as well as some bunkers dug into the side of hills. Mostly though, we saw a bunch of people riding bikes, as well as entrances to the beach that can be accessed if you have a surf fishing pass and a four-wheel drive vehicle. We had neither.

Finally, we got to the end of the road at a place called Herring Point. We parked the car, and got out to explore a little. There was a split-rail fence at the edge of a steep hill where we had a great view of the ocean below. There was also a path that you could take to walk down the side of the hill to get to the ocean. We didn't do that.

"Hey Al" I yelled, "Let's see one of your famous cliff diving moves from here!"

"I'll tell you what, John, how about if I just toss you over the side and you can see it first hand, up close, and personal."

"Someone woke up on the wrong side of the bed! You still thinking about your aborted love rendezvous last night?'

Al just looked at me and flashed a quick smile.

"OK, boys" Bruce shouted. "Let's get this show on the road. North Carolina awaits!"

With that, we loaded up and continued our southward trip down the Delmarva Peninsula. The GPS told us we would be in Lumberton, North Carolina in about 7 hours and 15 minutes. My plan, however, called for a brief gas and meal stop in Selma, North Carolina, which conveniently was also the home to a large cigar outlet named JR's Cigars. That would definitely delay our arrival into Lumberton.

✳

Our southward drive down the peninsula was reminiscent of the drive between Dover and the beach towns. It was very rural... lots of farms interspersed with small towns where the speed limits would drop significantly until we got through the two or three traffic signals that were their most memorable attractions.

That was a bit rude. Kind of reminds me of the Manhattan snobs who like to disrespect Staten Island at every possible turn. I'll remind the other John of that later.

Other than a quick gas stop, we pushed through the three states that make up Delmarva, and finally reached the Chesapeake Bay Bridge Tunnel. An engineering marvel if there ever was one.

The name – Chesapeake Bay Bridge Tunnel – accurately describes exactly what it is... a 17.6-mile span across the mouth of the Chesapeake Bay, made up of a combination of bridges and tunnels. It connects the southern tip of Delmarva, which is the portion of the peninsula that belongs to Virginia, to the Virginia Beach and Hampton Roads areas of Virginia proper. It was really a fascinating portion of the trip, and one we weren't expecting since none of us gave this leg much in the way of research. We transitioned from tunnel to bridge and back to tunnel again several time before reaching Hampton, Virginia.

The GPS guided us past the Norfolk Naval Base

where we were able to get a quick glance at several warships, including a couple of aircraft carriers. Beyond that, we headed west, which would put us back on Interstate 95 South as we rolled toward North Carolina.

I think that our brief sighting of the ships at the Norfolk Naval Base planted a question in my mind. I decided to pose it to my companions.

"Hey, guys. Why do you think it is that none of us ever went into the military? I mean, several of our buddies from high school went in, but none of us ever did, and I can't even remember any of us even talking about it."

The others thought about this for a moment and it was Bruce who responded first.

"Well, all four of us were only teenagers, too young to be drafted, when the Vietnam War ended. The draft ended not long after that... so I would guess that had something to do with it. Other than that, my days of playing tin soldier were pretty much limited to my childhood."

"Yeah, OK, but the end of the draft didn't keep some of our classmates from joining." I continued. "And we could have received good career training from the military, not to mention the GI Bill benefits we could have received."

Alfred spoke next.

"Well, that's true, but I can only speak for myself

about not enlisting. The Vietnam War was disproportionately represented by African American soldiers who were drafted. Not a lot of college deferments, or rich daddies to keep them out of it. That didn't go over very well in my family. There were a lot of negative comments about that whenever we had gatherings with our extended family." He took a deep breath and finished his thought. "That played a big part in me not going into the military."

Mark then said that he didn't go in because he had been working in the restaurant even back in high school and ever since then, he knew what he wanted to do.

"Was the military going to teach me how to run a restaurant in New York? How to hire good help... how to manage the budget and keep the place stocked? Hell no! My best training was right here."

"That makes sense." I said. "The reasons from all three of you makes perfect sense."

"What about you, John?" asked Bruce. "Why didn't you go in?"

"Damn. I wish I had as good an answer as you guys. To be honest though, I really don't know. I guess the best I can say is that I never gave it much thought and once my cousin got me the job at Con Ed, it just made sense for me to continue with that."

Bruce offered more thoughts on the subject.

"Let's not forget things like the secret bombings in

Cambodia, the My Lai Massacre, and of course, Kent State. Nixon was a disaster, and all of this crap combined to turn me off to anything government-related."

The rest of us agreed with his comments and the discussion faded soon thereafter. However, I continued to toss around the topic in my head. When I initially asked my friends about the military, I failed to first work through the question in my own mind. My lack of preparation probably had a lot to do with my response. One which I now consider to be fairly superficial. Yes, I had a good job at Con Ed, but did it really have anything to do with me not going into the military? No, it didn't. That was just a quickly fabricated response on my part to get off the hook. I was avoiding answering the question honestly. While it's true that the military would have given me good job training and a chance to see a lot of the world, I would never have risked what I already had in my life. I felt then, as I do now, that I had everything I needed, the most important being the three guys that were in the car with me. These guys have the ability to make me crazy, for sure, but our group is tight-knit. In a way, we're brothers. No, that's wrong. We're closer than any brothers I know. We're inseparable and THAT is why I never went into the military. I'm certain that this also played an important part in my friends' decisions to pass on the military. However, none of us wanted to say that we didn't go in because it would have meant leaving the group, even if only for a few years. That would have led to swift and well-deserved mockery from the others. But it was true. It was very true. I kept this truth to myself and drove on.

It wasn't too long before we reached I-95, not far from the Carolina border in Emporia, Virginia. Here we turned south once again. According to the GPS, we were about one hour and thirty minutes until we reached Selma, North Carolina, home to the JR Cigars outlet. I brought the speed of the car up to 80 mph, hoping to shave a few minutes off of the arrival time. Every car around me must have been going there as well, since I wasn't passing anyone. I even had a couple of cars speed by me rapidly. They were easily pushing a 100 mph. I wasn't in that much of a hurry, and I was confident JR Cigars wouldn't run out of supplies before we got there. We pulled into the outlet parking lot around 6:30pm.

Before we got out of the car, I offered a suggestion.

"OK guys… it will be tempting to spend a lot of money in this place but I think we should be careful not to do that. Bruce, you told me that Key West is full of cigar stores and open-air shops selling cigars, right?"

"That's right. When I was researching Key West online, multiple people talked about how there are cigar shops all over the place."

"OK, that's what I thought. So, how about if we just

buy one box of 20 cigars to start us off, and then we'll just buy more in Key West as needed. We can get a box of Cohiba's Blue for a couple hundred dollars, so about $50 each."

Alfred was in the back seat and leaned forward. "Definitely. We're just a couple of days into this trip so let's not blow our money too soon."

Mark agreed. "Yeah, one box of Cohiba's, and we roll. Ten minutes, in and out."

Bruce didn't say anything, but his body language showed agreement as we exited the car. Stepping into that place was amazing. It was huge and the entire place was one big humidor. I could have spent the rest of the day in there, but our agreement was fresh on my mind. We were in there more than ten minutes, but it was not more than thirty or forty minutes. I was very happy about that. When we left, we had our cigar stash in-hand, and we were once again southward bound. The GPS showed we only had another hour and a half to our next overnight stop at Lumberton, North Carolina. By 8pm, it was rapidly chirping away with directions to our hotel, a Motel 6 right off the highway.

Now… I can tell you in all sincerity that from what we could see of Lumberton from the highway, and then from our hotel, it was something less than impressive. The Motel 6 was even less so. That being said, it was fine for a one-night stop, and I would be willing to bet that Lumberton has a lot more to offer than what we could see from our I-95 exit. I've heard that these smaller towns that are near interstates, typically have nice main streets and historic districts that people flying by on the interstates rarely see.

We ate dinner at a nearby Cracker Barrel, followed by a stop at a small bar with a couple of pool tables. This was all we really needed to enjoy ourselves. We broke up into teams of two, and tied up one of the pool tables for about three hours before calling it a day. The one thing I think I'll remember most about Lumberton was how friendly everyone was we encountered there. The receptionist at the hotel, the young guy at the gas station, and the bartender where we shot pool, were all enjoyable to talk with and seemed to go out of their way to make us feel welcome. This must be what people are referring to when they talk about southern hospitality. I guess, after all, this is the most important characteristic of any town.

For this stop, I would room with Bruce, with Al and Mark taking the second room. For some reason, Bruce seemed apologetic about this stop as we were settling in for the night.

"Not the greatest place, is it?"

"It's fine, man! We all agreed that we only needed a clean place to stay that was affordable. Nothing fancy. We're all tired and it would have been a mistake to try and push on any further. I'm very satisfied with this place, and I haven't heard any complaints from the others either."

"Yeah, I guess… but I was just wondering if I could have found a better hotel for us in the area."

I tried to sooth his anxiety a bit.

"Well, you can worry about that if you need to, but I really think this was a good choice. We'll let you know if you screw up. You know that's true."

"Yeah, I sure do. Subtlety is not a strength in this group. And it was sure nice when Mark and I beat you and Al like redheaded stepchildren at the pool table tonight!"

"Shut the hell up and go to sleep. I normally wouldn't have let you guys beat us, but I felt sorry for you since you were obviously upset about picking such a shitty stop."

He laughed as he reached to turn off the lamp. It couldn't have been more than five minutes before we were both snoring.

7 - DAY THREE

October 16th

The next morning, we were all up and ready to go by 9AM. I guess everyone was more than ready to exchange Lumberton for Daytona Beach. We didn't stick around for the free breakfast, deciding to just grab some Egg McMuffins and coffee to-go from the local McDonald's. Bruce took his turn behind the wheel. Assuming we stopped somewhere for lunch, the trip to Daytona would probably be between seven and eight hours depending on traffic.

Shortly after leaving Lumberton, we approached a place called South of the Border, which, as the name implies, is just south of the North Carolina – South Carolina border. We'd been seeing crazy signs on the highway for this place for miles. Based on what we saw of this place from the highway, the signs were just the preamble to the craziness. Bruce spotted it first.

"Take a look at this place guys. That giant sombrero is the end of the rainbow for all of those signs we were passing yesterday and this morning."

It looked like something out of the past. Think of a cluster of bad motels mixed with off-brand fast-food joints and gaudy souvenir shops that I could only imagine were filled with treasures such as giant fly swatters, lewd post cards, kitchen magnets, and straw sombreros, all made in China. I had a smirk on my face when I gave my opinion.

"As much as I would love to explore this Mecca, maybe we should just skip it this time."

Al was less generous.

"What a dump! Don't even slow the car down, Bruce."

"Don't worry about that – I have no intention of going anywhere near that place!"

Bruce accelerated to around 80 mph to help make his point, and we all settled in for what promised to be a long and somewhat boring drive to Daytona. I noticed Mark was already closing his eyes after finishing his sausage biscuit and hash browns, and I thought he had the right idea. Still, I couldn't help but stay awake and take in the whole experience… even if it consisted mostly of pine trees, billboards, and tractor trailers. The thought of being in Daytona Beach by dinner time was exciting. Bruce said the hotel we would be staying at, another Motel 6, was right next to the Daytona Speedway. We were all anxious to see that, as well as the beach itself, of course.

We passed exit signs for places we had heard of like Charleston, Hilton Head, and Savannah... and a whole lot more for places we had never heard of like Manning, Summerton, and Beaufort. The signs were the closest we came to seeing any of them from our vantage point on Interstate 95. If we had an infinite amount of time and money to spend, I would have liked to see most of those places. Well... at least the ones I'd heard of. But time and money were both scarce commodities, so onward we pushed through South Carolina and through Georgia. We crossed into Florida at around 3pm.

It's hard to explain how I felt about being in Florida. I'd heard so much about it, both good and bad. The beaches, Disney, Miami, the Keys all stacking up on the 'good-side.' Hurricanes, hanging chads, alligators, and insects the size of small dogs on the 'bad-side.' Of course, I haven't seen any of these yet, so I can't speak with any credibility to either the good or the bad. Everything I knew about Florida came from TV and from previous travelers who told me their stories... but all of that was about to change. My buddies and I were about to experience it first-hand, and I couldn't have been happier about that. This trip has already been filled with 'firsts' and that streak would certainly continue until we were back on Staten Island.

We pulled into Daytona around 7:30pm; much later

than we thought we would. There was an accident that slowed things down considerably just south of Jacksonville. After we got through it, we decided to stop for a late lunch, which turned into a nearly two-hour affair, partly because of slow service and partly because we spent a lot of time talking about everything under the sun. For a second, I thought Mark was going to spring his news to the others about getting married. Alfred made a reference to the waitress wearing a wedding ring and speculated on whether she was really married or just wearing the ring to deter unwanted advances. She had all of the credentials for such an advance. This spurred Bruce to throw out a comment about not understanding why anyone feels the need to get married. Mark snickered at that and then spoke up.

"Well," … (it was precisely here that my hopes soared) … "my guess is because of the tax advantages." …and then they crashed.

The hotel was perfect for us. It was right next to the Speedway, which was impressive from the outside. We were several miles from the ocean but that was OK. Our plan was to check-in, grab a quick meal, and find a place for a night-cap. We also wanted to make it an early night since we had a full schedule the next day. Well, you know what they say about plans.

Yes, I do! It was John Lennon who said "Life is what

happens to you while you are busy making other plans."

We got out of the car, grabbed the luggage, and started to walk towards the entrance. After only a few steps, I realized I had forgotten my coffee thermos in the car.

"Shit. Hey, Bruce, let me have the car keys. I left my thermos in the car. Take my bag in and I'll meet you guys in the lobby."

Bruce tossed me the keys and Mark took my bag. They went into the lobby while I went to retrieve my coffee. It was exactly where I left it on the passenger side floorboard. I grabbed it, and as I slammed the car door shut, I had a sudden sinking feeling. I quickly felt the outside of my pockets and realized I didn't have the keys. Apparently, when I had leaned into the car to pick up the thermos, I set the keys down in the drink holder. Then without thinking, I instinctively pushed down on the manual door lock just before closing the door. The keys were locked in the car. I cursed myself, and thought about how much hell I was going to catch for this.

Now – that in and of itself was bad enough, but things only got worse from there. After confirming that all the doors of the car were indeed locked, I heard someone come up behind me. I assumed it was one of my buddies, but I was very wrong.

"Give me your car keys and your wallet, asshole."

I turned to find a guy who looked about thirty years old with a scruffy beard, baseball hat, black t-shirt, and jeans. He was an inch or two shorter than me and average weight, maybe 175-180 pounds. He was holding what looked like a hunting knife with a long blade. I couldn't believe this is the way our first night in Florida was starting.

"Hey, man, you're not going to believe this, but I just locked my keys in the car. Can you give me a break here?"

"Bullshit... give me the keys or I'm going to use this knife and take the keys myself."

I needed to stall. "OK, just listen for a second. You can look in the car and see the keys for yourself. I just got here and I accidently locked them in the car when I came back for my thermos. You gotta believe me."

He took a quick glance into the car but stayed close enough to be within striking distance with that knife. He obviously saw the keys; his frustration was apparent.

"Give me your wallet."

"Uh boy. Well, that's something else you're not going to be happy about. I have no cash. Zero dollars. I've only got one credit card. I can give it to you but I need my driver's license and other stuff in the wallet."

His agitation clearly grew as he tried to figure out in his pea-brain what his options were for a next step.

Luckily for me, his brain worked slowly, and I have very impatient friends. I didn't need to stall any longer.

"Hey, John, you have a new friend?" It was Mark.

The intended thief was startled and turned around in a quick jerking motion to see Mark, Al and Bruce standing about 10 feet away.

"Yeah, I didn't catch his name, but he's interested in taking your car, and my wallet out for a spin."

Mark laughed. "Well, I don't care about your wallet, but he's not taking my car anywhere."

Al shook his head and spoke up.

"I don't think I'll let him take your wallet either, John. I was counting on you to pay for my drinks tonight, and you're not going to get off that easy."

Al looked into the would-be assailant's eyes for a second, and then looked back at me.

"Stretcher or bag, John?"

Knife-Man's face showed confusion and concern. Even an idiot can sometimes tell when the tide turns.

"I don't know Al. Let me ask him." I stared at the guy and translated for him.

"My friend is asking if I want you to leave on a stretcher or in a bag. But I'm thinking there may also be a third option. I can see a way that you may actually be able to walk away from this. Of course, that would require you to give up trying to get my keys and wallet. So, how do you think we should proceed here? Do you think you might want to walk away from this in one piece? Your call."

He was confused, angry and scared. I saw all three in his eyes. He finally responded.

"Fuck you guys." He started to back away, hoping to identify an escape route.

"Language, language, blockhead. You're not fucking us or anyone else tonight," I said. "And by the way, you're not going anywhere with that knife."

There was no way we were going to let him terrorize someone else nearby with that knife. He now had a new look in his eyes. He was intimidated. Panic was building inside of him.

As Mark, Bruce, and Al slowly moved to block his desired exit, I tried to help him understand his options one more time.

"Do I have to draw you a picture, moron? If you drop the knife, we'll let you leave in one piece. If you try to keep it, we'll be forced to take it from you; but if you choose that path, you won't be able to walk anywhere for a very long time. This I promise you."

He was now sweating profusely and struggling to keep all four of us within his field of vision. He stood very still for a minute. His shoulders slumped and he took a deep breath. The resignation in his body language was unmistakable. He dropped his knife to the ground.

Al was angry and started moving toward the source

of that anger. That was potentially very bad for Ex-Knife Man who noticed the closing distance between them. With his artificial courage now laying safely on the ground, he showed his true colors with an indecipherable scream as he ran away in panic. It looked like Mark and Bruce were about to give chase, but I called them off.

"Let him go, guys. He isn't worth it."

I picked up the knife and we all started walking back toward the hotel. I dropped the knife in the trash can outside the entrance and put my hand on the back of Alfred's neck. "Let's check-in pal."

When we entered the lobby, Alfred snapped his fingers and stopped. He asked me for the car keys since he was on deck for driving duty.

I thought to myself "Oh crap… the keys!"

This wasn't going to be good.

"Oh yeah. Well…"

They all looked at me inquisitively as I grasped for words.

"There's one more thing I've got to tell you guys. Let's grab a cigar and meet out front. I'll explain it to you."

8 - DAY FOUR

October 17th

By the time we woke up the next morning, we'd all but forgotten about the pathetic Knife-Man. The same could not be said about the keys being locked in the car. Even though it really wasn't a big deal, Al assured me it wouldn't take him long to get into the car, the trash-talk that I received from the others was relentless. While Mark, Bruce and I grabbed our carb-heavy breakfast and coffee offered by the hotel, Alfred took a wire hanger, given to him by one of the hotel staff, and as promised, had the car opened and keys retrieved in about ten minutes. Still, there was no way the ease of retrieval was going to be taken into consideration by my three comrades. The mockery lasted about an hour.

"OK, OK, I deserve the abuse. Yes, it was a lame-brained thing to do. Now get off my ass guys or I'll resign as your entertainment director. And that would be too bad for all of you because I have a big day planned."

Bruce got in one final shot before the truce. "OK keyless. We'll forgive you because of your mental disorder, but this better be one hell of a day to make up for it!"

I actually did have a great day planned. We would start with a tour at the Daytona International Speedway, something Alfred and I were most interested in seeing. That would last about an hour. After that, we would spend some time driving on the beach and seeing what trouble we could get into there. I got the big thumbs-up from all three for both activities. But I also had a surprise planned that we hadn't previously talked about at all. Everything we had done up to this point had been a new experience for us. (Well, other than the attempted robbery. That kind of thing wasn't completely new for us.) We were seeing things we never thought we would ever see, and we were making memories that would last for the rest of our lives. But with this surprise, I was really stepping out of the box. Before we left to go to the track, I told them what I wanted to do.

"Hey, guys. There's one more thing that I want us to do today. Actually, it would be tonight."
They were intrigued.

"There's a town about a half-hour from here named Cassadaga. It's known as the "Psychic Capital of the World." because of how many psychics and mediums live there. I say we go and have our fortunes told… or whatever it is they call it."

"Where did you hear about this place?" Mark asked.

"From a coworker who has a cousin that lives around here somewhere, and knew all about it. So, I did some research before we left Staten Island and it all checked out. There are lots of people who are convinced this is all legitimate."

Bruce was skeptical, not only about the legitimacy of the place, but also about even being able to just walk in and get a session with somebody. I was way ahead of him for once.

"True Bruce, but I was hopeful that you guys would be interested in doing this, so I went ahead and got us a reservation for 7pm tonight. I got a lady who is supposedly a highly regarded psychic and had great reviews online. Regardless of how real this stuff is or isn't, I think it would be fun to hear what she might have to say about us."

At that point, both Mark and Bruce agreed to go, but not before Bruce asked if the psychic was cute. His question was met only with eye rolls.

Alfred had been quietly taking in the conversation and finally spoke up.

"I don't know, man. I don't think it's a good idea to play around with that kind of stuff. I believe there are some things we don't understand, and we probably shouldn't poke around in it like it's some kind of child's game."

"OK, fair enough, Al" I said. "But let's not rule it out right now. Let's go ahead and do the speedway, and the beach, and we can make a final decision about Cassadaga afterward."

Alfred was obviously uneasy about having Cassadaga still being on the table, but he agreed so we could get the day rolling. We piled into the car with Alfred behind the wheel, and made the two-minute trip across the road to the Daytona Speedway.

The place was huge. Much larger than any of us were expecting. It had a modern look to it and it was beautifully landscaped with palm trees and a large pond out front.

"Jeez, take a look at this place!" Alfred said. "You think they take in some money here?" he asked sarcastically.

"No kidding," Mark responded. "Unbelievable. I'd love to have the pizza and sub concession here."

We were there a little early and just about the first ones in line for the tour. It was better than any of us expected. We watched a short movie about the history of NASCAR, which was fascinating, and we got to see the winning car of the last Daytona 500. The name of the driver was displayed on a plaque beside the car. I didn't recognize the name. Like I said earlier, I'm not a big NASCAR fan. We were then ferried onto a tram that took us out on the track. I don't know what I was expecting, but that track was awe inspiring. I thought the inside of Yankee Stadium was big, but this place dwarfed that landmark. The tour guide told us the track is 2.5 miles long and the banks on each corner are sloped at 31 degrees, allowing the cars to take the corners at nearly 200 mph.

Impressive unless you compare it to the New Jersey Turnpike near MetLife Stadium after a Giants game.

I believe Alfred was the most impressed. I suspect his mechanical prowess had a lot to do with that. Bruce was more into the track design, and the high level of engineering technology that was described in the film at the onset of the tour. Even Mark, who typically has very little interest in sports outside of his favorite New York teams, seemed to enjoy this tour. By the time our hour was up, we all walked out of that place with a newfound respect for NASCAR racing. Make no mistake, we would still prefer to go to a baseball or football game, but we certainly understood why NASCAR is so popular.

Next up was a drive to the beach, just about three miles away from the track. The beach is lined with hotels and condominiums of all shapes, sizes, and obviously, price ranges. Daytona Beach is twenty-three miles long and very wide. The white sand is hardpacked, making it drivable without the need for a four-wheel drive vehicle. Even though it was October, the temperature was warm for us, but cooler than normal for Floridians. We paid the $25.00 fee and drove onto 'The World's Most Famous Beach' as the locals like to call it.

"Where to boys?" asked Alfred as we rolled onto the sand.

It wasn't like there were many options. We could either go north or south without ending up in the ocean. Before responding, I pointed south for no particular reason, other than to avoid driving into the ocean. I then shrugged my shoulders, and offered a dispassionate opinion.

"Nowhere special. Let's just drive for a while and see what we can see. After that, we can go back up to A1A and find a place to park so we can walk along the boardwalk."

Al piped in when he heard that. "Yeah! Maybe we can find a place that sells corn dogs and French fries."

"Now you're talking!" opined Bruce.

We drove for several miles. We stopped a couple of times just to stick our feet in the ocean, or watch some people surf fishing. One guy even pulled in a baby shark, maybe eighteen inches long, while we watched. After carefully… very carefully… removing the hook from the shark's mouth using a pair of pliers, the guy threw the shark back into the surf.

Note to self – Stay out of the ocean in Florida! If there are baby sharks around, the mamma and pappa sharks probably aren't too far away.

We were hoping to see a few more bikinis than we did, but given the cooler than normal day with overcast skies, there weren't too many people on the beach. The few people we did see swimming were even whiter than me (That's saying something!), so we guessed they were Canadians, who love to come to Florida during the colder months. I noticed that several of the hotels along the strip flew both American and Canadian flags out front. The locals call the northerners who head south during the winter 'snowbirds'.

We were on the beach for about an hour before deciding to leave the sand and surf behind, using an access ramp leading back to the hardtop. We headed north on A1A hoping to find a parking lot or garage near the Boardwalk. There were a few places to park but we found one that was close to the boardwalk pier. The pier juts out a thousand feet from the beach. It's the only pier I've ever seen that includes a restaurant. We walked to the end of the pier where fishermen had their lines in the water, and where hundreds of people of all varieties walked with their dogs, or children, or hand-in-hand with each other. Everyone clearly enjoyed the bright sun and the crashing waves.

The boardwalk itself was surprisingly small for such a large beach, just over a mile long. Still, there was plenty to keep us busy. We hit the area south of the pier first, which had the rides and a classic arcade. The four of us enjoyed the old-school pinball machines and Skee-Ball games. This kept us at each other's throats for a good two-hours. Nothing like some games to bring out our overly-competitive natures. It reminded us of our neighborhood Monopoly wars.

After we were all hoarse from the loud trash talk, we headed north on the boardwalk to check out the historic bandshell that was built between 1936 and 1937. It was empty when we were there, but interesting to see. I checked on my cellphone, and read that the bandshell is known for its annual free summer concerts. It has hosted everyone from Blake Shelton to Buddy Guy to Huey Lewis & The News. I thought about how much fun it would be to attend a concert at that location. I wondered what it would be like to hear the music merging with the sounds of the crashing waves. It must be a unique and memorable experience.

At that point, we'd had about enough of the beach, but before leaving we each pigged out on corn dogs and fries, and followed up with our Cohibas. That made us all very happy! We decided to nurse our "carb comas" at the hotel, so we headed back. Along the way, we took advantage of Alfred's full stomach, getting him to agree to make the trip to get our psychic reading at Cassadaga. It would take us about a half an hour to get there from the hotel. That meant we could rest up until about 6pm, giving us a chance to take our time getting there in case we somehow got lost, or wanted to see something along the way.

$$*$$

We didn't get lost and there wasn't really anything that enticed us to stop along the way. I found it interesting how quickly Florida transitions from city to rural scrublands. We drove past miles of these palmetto and pine tree covered areas, passing only small stands on the side of the road selling fruit or boiled peanuts. It's very scenic, and very different from anything on Staten Island, but there was certainly no reason to make any stops. That was fine.

Just curious... why would anyone want to boil a peanut? I've never heard of that. I'm going to have to google that later to find out.

We got to Cassadaga at about 6:30pm and just drove around taking it all in. It was a nice little town with mostly wood-frame cottages, a small hotel, a few parks, a post office, and a few restaurants. We decided to head over to the psychic medium's address a little before 7pm.

The address led to an old but well-maintained house with a large porch, home to several rocking chairs and hummingbird feeders. The sign hanging on the etched glass front door invited us in. We entered a small room with several eclectic chairs lining two of the walls and a young lady sitting at a simple wooden desk containing only a 1960's vintage AT&T Harvest Gold telephone and an iPad. It was photo worthy, but I dared not. The young lady asked if she could help us. I stepped forward.

"Hello. We have a reservation with Catherine Millings."

"Then this must be the Schumacher party, yes?"

"Yes Ma'am, we are."

"OK great. Have a seat and I'll inform her of your arrival."

We all sat, with the exception of Alfred. He still seemed a little on edge about coming to this place, and he just walked around the room looking at pictures, and picking up and setting down a few trinkets on some shelving. I didn't think there was anything left about Alfred that would ever surprise me, but his reticence to this experience did just that. He showed not the slightest bit of fear facing a guy with a knife the previous night, but in this room, his anxiety was palpable. I was going to say something, but then thought it would be best to just pretend I didn't notice.

The receptionist returned to the room about five minutes later and told us Ms. Millings was ready to see us. She waved us toward the hallway and said we should go to the last room on the right. As we entered the room, Catherine Millings greeted us and shook each of our hands as we introduced ourselves. She invited us to have a seat. There were two large leather couches in the room that faced an overstuffed chair. We sat on the couches as she settled into the chair. I recognized her from her online photos, but they must have been taken several years prior because she looked older than the photos suggested. I guessed her age to be about 55, and she was quite elegant with a brown and yellow striped dress, adorned with a gold chain necklace and several gold bangled bracelets. Her hair was starting to show hints of silver and it was beautifully styled.

There was about a minute of awkward silence as she appeared to be assessing us as well. She made eye contact with each of us individually before speaking up.

"So, gentleman... how can I help you?"

The four of us looked at each other, hoping one of us was prepared to answer that question. It was obvious none of my comrades were prepared to do so. I guessed it would be up to me. Fair enough, since this was all my idea.

"Well, to be honest with you Ms. Millings…"

"Please. Call me Catherine."

"Thank you. To be honest Catherine, this is our first experience with this type of thing, and we don't really know what we want, other than to listen to what you might have to say about us. Sorry… this probably sounds strange to you."

She responded quickly while waving off my response with her hand. "Not at all! Everyone has to start somewhere with any new experience. I'm glad you are trusting me with your first step into the psychic realm. Please give me a second to prepare. I'll ask that each of you join me in silence as I do so."

We complied. She lowered her head for what was probably only about a minute, but it seemed much longer. She raised her head but continued her silence. I suspect this made the others as uncomfortable as it made me. I noticed after a few minutes that the expression on her face changed. When we first came in, and prior to asking for silence, her face seemed relaxed and serene with a slight smile that served to relax me. Now, however, her face was screaming confusion. Her eyes were bouncing back and forth between the four of us as if she were watching a tennis tournament. At one point, she closed her eyes again, as if trying to reset and start over. When she reopened them, the tennis match continued. Finally, she shook her head and stood up.

"Excuse me, gentlemen."

She went to the door and summoned the receptionist. Catherine told her to go next door and ask someone (I didn't catch the name) to come over immediately, if possible. She further explained to the receptionist that she needed some advice. Now it wasn't just Alfred who was anxious. The four of us looked at each other without saying a word, but clearly all in an equal state of bewilderment. Catherine returned her attention to us.

"I'm so sorry for the interruption, gentlemen. If you don't mind, I'd like to bring in a colleague. She's a mentor of mine, and very experienced. I'm not sure about something, and I want to get her advice."

It was Alfred who spoke for the group.

"What is it you are unsure about? What's wrong?"

"Oh, nothing is wrong. I'm seeing something that is unusual and I'm not sure if I'm having an off day, which happens sometimes, or if it's something else. My colleague will be able to help me clarify this."

That wasn't enough information for any of us. Bruce pushed a bit more.

"Something else – Like what?"

"I apologize, but please trust me. I'll answer all of your questions, but allow me to hear from my colleague first. She's right next door and will be here any second."

Catherine was exactly right about that. Seconds after making that statement, there was a knock at the door.

Catherine opened it and hugged the older lady who stood in the doorway. The older lady looked to be in her late 70s or early 80s, but she seemed very healthy and alert. Catherine then ushered her colleague out of the room, turning her head toward us as she was departing.

"We'll be right back, gentlemen. Promise."

The four of us sat dumbfounded.

"What the fuck is this all about?" Mark asked.

I shrugged my shoulders as Alfred raised his arms, and gave me the "I told you so" look. Bruce lent us his opinion.

"Maybe it's just part of the show. Maybe this is a way to draw us in... to make us a little nervous about spirits or something."

"Well, it's fucking working man." Alfred was clearly uncomfortable with all of this and I was afraid he would walk out, and none of us would be able to stop him if he made that decision.

Just then, Catherine walked back in the room with the elder woman who took the chair as Catherine stood beside her.

"Gentlemen, thank you for your patience. I'd like to introduce you all to my mentor and friend, Sasha Kobliska. She has agreed to help in this process." She turned to her colleague "Sasha, this is John, Mark, Alfred and Bruce."

"Good evening, sirs" Sasha said with a heavy Slavic

accent.

We nodded and returned the greeting. Sasha then followed the same procedure as Catherine did earlier, asking us for silence and dropping her head for a minute or two. And sure enough, when she opened her eyes and looked at us, the tennis match resumed. The difference between Catherine and Sasha, however, was that Sasha's smile replaced Catherine's look of confusion. I must admit, the smile made me feel a little bit better. Sasha looked at Catherine.

"It is not you, sweetheart. What you see is real."

Catherine nodded and smiled slightly herself. Sasha then asked Catherine if she wanted to take over or if she wanted her to maintain the lead. Catherine asked Sasha to continue, and then addressed the four of us.

"Gentlemen, with your permission, Sasha will take the lead while I observe. She is more experienced than myself, and under the circumstances, she will serve you better than myself."

I looked around at the others quickly and saw nothing but some shrugged shoulders. "Sure, please go ahead." Both ladies smiled and Sasha leaned forward in the chair.

"Sirs, thank you. I know we have confused you with all of this, so please allow me to explain. One of the things we do here with our customers is read auras. Every person has an aura. It is an energy field, or a luminous body that surrounds your physical body. Auras emit different colors, and these colors are a manifestation of your physical and spiritual body. The colors can be red, orange, yellow, etcetera, and depending on the color, we can predict if you are strong-willed, or energetic, or intuitive, or any one of many other human characteristics."

She stopped for a second, probably to give us a chance to ask a question. None of us, however, were ready to do that. We were eager to hear more. After waiting an appropriate amount of time for potential questions, and receiving none, she continued.

"Now, under normal conditions, when we meet with four people in a group like the four of you, we will see four individual auras. The auras may all be different colors... or some different and some the same, or they may even all be the same color, but regardless of any of this, the auras are separate and distinct for each individual person. This, however, is not true for the four of you."

I had a question. "Are you saying you don't see any auras for us?"

"No. What I'm saying is that the four of you share an aura. When we look at you, it's like a storm of colors bouncing between each of you. I've heard of this, but until today I had never actually experienced it. I thought it was just legend. Can I ask one of you to leave the room, please? It doesn't matter which one, and it will only be for a few seconds."

Bruce volunteered and stepped out of the room. Both Catherine and Sasha followed him out. In short order, all three returned to the room. Sasha continued her explanation.

"OK. What we just did was a quick experiment. When Mr. Bruce walked out of the room, Catherine and I saw what I will call fingers from a portion of the aura follow him out. Those fingers remained with him while he was outside the room and followed him back when he returned. The rest of you continued to have the aura all around you as it was previously. So, it appears that this one aura follows the four of you around, even when you are not together. Fascinating!"

I didn't know what to make of this and from the look on my friend's faces, I knew they were equally baffled. If this was an act… a ruse to disarm us so we would keep coming back… these ladies deserve an Oscar. I'm a natural skeptic. I look at everything with a suspicious eye, and I can spot a scam from a mile away. As I listened to these ladies, none of my warning flags were waving. I believed what they were telling us was true. I had to ask the obvious question.

"Sasha… Catherine… what are we to do with this information? I don't know what it means or what the significance is." Catherine responded first.

"I don't think there is anything to be done other than

to recognize that what the four of you have is a remarkable relationship. It's a relationship and a connectiveness like none that I have ever seen before, and will likely never see again."

Sasha then gave her thoughts. "My friend Catherine is correct. My advice to you is to treat it as a gift. I suspect you already knew you had something special between the four of you. Odd similarities, a closeness, and an understanding of one another that went beyond the norm. Perhaps the information we offered you tonight will help you understand why you are all so close. But I wonder if this knowledge should even matter to you at all. Does it really change anything? Each of you have a rare gift... the gift of each other. Never underestimate the value of that."

Alfred stood up. For a minute I thought he was going to leave, but instead, he turned to face us.

"I have never underestimated that value. I never will."

At that, we all came to our feet. It was a weird moment, and I never felt more emotionally stunted. The others must have felt the same way as we each went from one to the other fist bumping, high-fiving, and slapping each other on the back.

Catherine and Sasha observed this awkwardness and started laughing. It was Catherine who managed to verbalize what she saw.

"Oh yeah... they are all definitely cut from the same cloth!"

More laughter from both of them.

Our time was up and we said our good-byes, and gave both of these fascinating women our sincere thanks. They walked us to the front of the house where we entered earlier, and we all shook hands. But before we left, Sasha had one more surprise.

"There is something else. I hesitate to say anything because the image I am receiving is cloudy. Do you see it, Catherine?"

Catherine looked at us and then back to Sasha. "No, I don't."

"I'll share it with all of you if you promise not to push for an explanation or start asking a bunch of questions, for which I have no answers. Do you all agree?"

Everyone, including Catherine, nodded in agreement.

"Fine. I am seeing shadows of a future event. It portends an important moment in your lives; all four of you. I can't pinpoint how far in the future it will occur. It's not clear. But it is an event that will require a decision from each of you. Think of it as a fork in the road of life, and when you get to that fork, you will need to decide your direction. I regret I cannot offer you more than this. If I may borrow an expression from the Apostle Paul, I am looking through the glass darkly. My hope for each of you is that when that moment arrives, when you reach the fork, you will remember this conversation. All choices that we make in our lives are important, but for the four of you, this one seems to be particularly so, impacting the rest of your lives. Don't forget."

I thought about what she said and wanted to question her about it, but a deal is a deal. We promised not to ask. I simply responded with "Thank you for everything. I will never forget this experience. Goodbye."

The others each provided similar comments and thanks. Our time in the town of Cassadaga was over, but I suspect we will each carry what we saw and heard there within us for a long time. But for now, it was time to move on. We drove back to the hotel in near silence. We were all trying to process what we heard and what we were feeling. We had another long drive the next day to Miami, and I was hoping we would all be able to get some sleep. I wasn't betting on it.

✱

We got back to Daytona around 9:30pm. I was still pumped up about Cassadaga and decided it was too early for me to turn in. I sensed a restlessness in my friends as well, and I remembered the Cohiba's.

"Anyone up for a cigar? I noticed a sitting area out

back with some Adirondack chairs."

Not surprisingly, nobody was interested in hitting the sack, and everyone was interested in the cigars. Al retrieved them from the trunk of the car, while Mark went up to one of the rooms to grab four beers that we had left over from the previous day. We gathered like Knights of the Round Table to discuss the day, as well as whatever conquests lay ahead.

At first, there wasn't much more talk at all; similar to the drive back from Cassadaga. We cut the cigar ends, fired them up, and silently watched the smoke rise into the still night. At first, we were content with just that. A shared moment of peace. After a bit, I decided the time was right to address the elephant in the room.

"Damn, guys! I never saw that coming tonight."

I certainly didn't need to clarify my statement. Everyone knew exactly what I was talking about, and now we needed to work it out between us, as well as in our own heads. I was glad to have my friends with me, and eager to get their perspectives. Bruce responded to my comment.

"None of us saw it coming, John. I mean... first the aura thing, which seemed special, a gift they called it. And then on our way out the door, a type of warning that was so vague I don't know what to think about it."

Mark was next.

"Exactly. C'mon, some future event? A decision

that will impact our lives? She did use the word impact, right?"

"Yes, I'm pretty sure that's what Sasha said." I dug deeper into my memory. "But she had no idea when in the future, or anything about the decision that would need to be made. How are we supposed to be on the lookout for something that could be applied to almost any situation?"

"Yes!" Bruce said a little too loudly. "It's the stuff paranoia is made of. Think of the implications. Should I cross the street now? What if this is the important decision that was foretold to us in Cassadaga. Hell, it could make us go crazy."

Alfred took a big draw on his cigar, bent his neck all the way back, and slowly blew the smoke straight up.

"I wonder if the fork-in-the-road premonition is the wrong thing for us to focus on. Afterall, it's like you said, Bruce, that vision will make us crazy if we let it rule our lives. Hell, we make decisions every day, and any one of them can lead us to riches or to our downfall. No. I think the most important thing we heard tonight... the thing we should really focus on... is the aura."

"I think you're right, Al" I said. "I've never met four other people who've had as much in common as we do. How often are we finishing each other's sentences? I always assumed it was because we grew up together, and I'm sure that's part of it, but now I think there may be more to it. After what I heard tonight, I'm starting to believe that the four of us are together... that we've been friends for so many years, and that we're so in sync with one another, is preordained."

Mark contemplated that and responded with a half-whisper that we barely heard.

"Preordained."

We waited, thinking correctly that he had more to say.

"I guess there are all kinds of ways we can describe why we've been together for as long as any of us can remember. I suppose preordained fits as well as anything else. But I prefer to keep it simple. You guys know I can sometimes be hard to get along with."

We all had to smile at that particular understatement.

"And yet, I've never felt judged by any of you. You've all put up with my bullshit for as long as I can remember, and this means more to me than anything else. I can't explain the whole aura thing. If we share an aura like those ladies say, I'm good with that. And if that's extremely rare... damn near unheard of... well that doesn't surprise me in the least."

"Amen to that brother!" Al said it first. The rest of us repeated it. Amen indeed.

With our cigars burned down to nubs, and our brains not far behind, we decided to call it a night. Tomorrow we would be Miami-bound, but we would always remember this stop in Daytona and Cassadaga.

You just never know when life is going to hand you something precious. Of all the places the guys had planned for this trip, who would have believed that an after-thought, a little speck on the map called Cassadaga, would be so impactful? Sure, there was some skepticism, and even a dose of fear mixed in, but they kept themselves open to new possibilities, and it paid off. Good for them!

9 - DAY FIVE

October 18th

We gathered in the lobby at 9AM, and once again took advantage of the carb-loaded free breakfast. Al said he would drive for the first couple of hours of the trip, and then hand the reins over to Mark who would take us the rest of the way to Miami. We grabbed some coffee to-go and we were on our way.

About 30 minutes into the trip, Bruce made a suggestion that he had apparently been contemplating over the past 24 hours.

"Hey, guys, I was thinking about something, and wanted to toss it out for a vote."

Alfred gave him the green light. "Toss away, man."

"Well, I've been thinking about Miami. I'm sure it's a great place, but I'm wondering if we should skip it."

Since I was the one who suggested a change to our plan by adding a trip to Cassadaga at the last minute, I should have been the one least entitled to a rapid push-back. But hell, that's never stopped me in the past.

"What are you talking about Bruce? Besides Key West, Miami was one of the places I thought we would like best. It's a big city with a lot going on."

"That's exactly why I think we should skip it. Look, we know big cities as well or better than almost anyone on this planet. I thought the idea of this trip was to experience new things. And we've done that up to this point, but I'm not sure Miami fits into that mold."

Mark jumped in. "What are you saying, Bruce? Do you think we should drive directly to Key West today?"

"No. I think we should push just a little beyond Miami and spend the night in Key Largo. I can call from my cellphone to change our reservations if you all agree."

"Well, I don't know if I agree or not," said Alfred. "Do we know anything about Key Largo? What are we going to do there? Oh, and by the way, what about those Cuban sandwiches we were going to get in Miami?"

The way to a man's heart is through his stomach is a saying that is particularly true of Alfred! I don't know how someone can eat so much and stay so fit.

Bruce thought he perceived a slight chink in our armor and he was ready with his counter-attack.

"Yes, I googled Key Largo yesterday before we left for Cassadaga. I like the idea of spending a night on one of the Keys other than Key West. Let me answer the easy question first. Key West is just 90 miles from Cuba. I've read that Key West has some of the best Cuban sandwiches anywhere, and you can eat them to your hearts content once we get there."

Then Bruce hit us with the big guns. "And... you're never going to believe what they have in Key Largo."

We looked at each other in silence, knowing full well that guesses would be fruitless. Mark decided to accelerate the discussion.

"Are you going to tell us, or do I have to beat it out of you?"

"The African Queen!"

We had no idea that Bruce was talking about.

"The movie?" I asked.

"No. The actual boat that was used in the movie is sitting in Key Largo waiting for us! They book it out for short cruises on the canal it sits on."

Now one thing I need to explain, especially to our younger readers, is that guys of a certain age... mature gentleman... love anything Humphrey Bogart related. They (we) grew up watching his movies on Saturday mornings and dreaming of being him with our arms around Lauren Bacall or Ingrid Bergman. 'The Maltese Falcon', 'Casablanca', and yes, 'The African Queen', and 'Key Largo' were, and still are, considered can't-miss movies whenever they are on TV.

This gave everyone pause. We were all pretty much ready to tell Bruce to go pound sand, and remain on course for Miami, but now… well, now what?

Here is where my pride got in the way. Looking back on it now, I can see that I became defensive about the self-perceived assault on my glorious travel plan. Just the day before, I made a change to that same plan, but that was different. You see, it was OK for me to change my plan, but for someone else to do it was blasphemy!

"No, I just don't think we should bypass Miami, Bruce. Sorry."

Alfred and Mark looked at each other and nodded. I knew I was in trouble. Alfred, being the better diplomat, decided he could soften my stance.

"I'm for passing up Miami and spending the night in Key Largo. Sorry John, but I REALLY want to see the African Queen. I think you do, too."

Bruce could see the tide was turning his way, so he remained quiet, but Mark wanted to add his vote in support of the change.

"Yeah, I want to see it too, John. How many times have we all sat together and watched that movie? There's no way we should miss taking a ride on it. As for Miami, I'm happy to make the trade."

Bruce listened and decided to add one final thought.

"John, you said yesterday that our friendship was preordained, and I agree. But with the African Queen being a shared experience in our lives, don't you think that we really have to go see it? Isn't it possible that going to Key Largo to see it is also preordained for us?"

I sat silently digesting what my friends were saying. In all honesty, I have to admit that my ego was still a little bruised, but I also knew they were speaking the truth. It was our truth. I responded in a soft voice.

"Yes. You guys are right. Let's go see the old girl."

With that, Bruce gave me a pat on the shoulder and was immediately on his cell making the necessary changes to our hotel reservations. He cancelled the one in Miami, and found a relatively inexpensive place on Key Largo. We programmed the new address into the GPS and it only added a little less than an hour to our original destination. We would arrive there around 3pm, so Bruce called to see if he could get us on a cruise sometime after that. Otherwise, we could reserve a cruise for the next morning. Surprisingly, there was an opening at 4pm and we jumped on it. We had no time to waste! African Queen – Here we come!

✳

Alfred took us as far as Vero Beach, where we gassed up the car, and Mark took the wheel from there. Traffic and congestion were definitely building the closer we got to Miami. We didn't realize how many beach towns we would drive through (or at least near) in South Florida. We passed so many, I can't remember all of them. Some that I can remember are Port St. Lucie, West Palm Beach, Delray Beach, Pompano Beach, Fort Lauderdale, and finally Miami. We were still on Interstate 95 the entire way until we passed Miami, where the southward road transitioned into Route 1. Prior to this, I realized (without saying anything to the others) that I was now glad we skipped Miami. Don't get me wrong, it looked like a great town, and I'm sure we would have had a good time, but it wasn't really meant to be part of our group adventure. Key Largo now felt right to me, and I'm grateful that my friends helped me to see that. And the African Queen... Ah yes... the African Queen.

We reached the city of Homestead. The landscape was similar to what we had been seeing all through South Florida, but upon our departure from that city, the world changed. We had entered a small portion of the Everglades that formed the southern tip of the Florida mainland just before entering the Keys. Unlike Miami, the Everglades wetlands offered us a glimpse into something totally foreign to us. In this flat water-world, we could see a 360-degree horizon, broken only by the occasional Cyprus trees or scrub oaks adorned with Spanish Moss. All four of us had our noses pressed against the car windows. And then, without any warning, Mark hit the brakes hard. Had it not been for the Taurus's anti-lock brakes, we would have likely skidded off the road. He pulled the car over.

"What the hell, man!" I shouted from the back seat.

Mark responded quickly with excitement in his voice.

"Look on the right side of the car in the grass... about 20 yards ahead!"

It was an alligator. At that moment, it looked as big as the car, but after we caught our breaths, it was probably between seven and eight feet long. It didn't move and neither did we. We just stared at it in disbelief; a clear indication that we were from New York, not Florida. Alfred clicked a couple of pictures from his iPhone. A couple of cars also traveling south went by us without even slowing down. This gave us time to think and talk this through.

"What do you guys want to do?" I asked. Then I clarified a bit. "Should we just be on our way or do you want to watch to see if it moves?"

Bruce let out a slightly nervous laugh and asked the next obvious question.

"Why isn't he moving? He's just sitting there watching us like he's waiting for us to make the first move."

Alfred joined in.

"I got a bunch of pictures of him. If he would move, I'd also take a video but he doesn't seem to be in a hurry to go anywhere. I say we just get going again."

Mark then threw down a challenge.

Of course, it had to be Mark!! Sometimes I wonder if he's slightly off.

"One of us has to get out of the car and walk toward him while Alfred takes the video. I'm sure that will make him run. The guys back on Staten Island won't believe it! We have to get this on video."

That was barely out of Mark's mouth before Bruce was all over it.

"Are you out of your mind? Look at the size of that thing. If any of us get too close to it, we'll be lunch!"

Alfred was nodding his head but didn't say anything.

I wanted to agree with Bruce. Stepping out of the car clearly involved risk. But something was holding me back. Something in my memory that I was desperately trying to retrieve but struggled to remember. It finally came to me. I rejoined the conversation.

"You can't steal second base while your foot is on first base."

The car fell silent. My friends looked at me with confusion and concern. Looking back on it now, they probably thought the madness that started with Mark was contagious and I too was now infected. After a few seconds, Al asked me what I was babbling about.

"It's a quote. I can't remember who said it, but I always thought it was true. It means that there are times when you have to take risks. Mark is right. One of us needs to get out of the car to see if we can get it to move."

Bruce: "I'm not believing this."

"No, hear me out" I said. "That thing is huge, so it's probably slow. If one of us can scare it without getting too close, we could catch it running off on video. That would be one hell of a video. One that we could bring back to New York and watch for years. I really think the risk is minimal and justifiable."

For the record, in a short distance, an alligator is as fast as a quarter-horse. If it wants you, it can run you down. I'm not surprised John, Mark and Al didn't know that, but I'm surprised about Bruce not picking up on it.

Everyone thought about what I said and let it soak in for a minute. Al needed less time than the rest of us before responding.

"I think it's a bad idea. I'm not getting out of the car and I don't think anyone else should either."

Mark then blurted out his decision without waiting for an alternative volunteer. "I'll go."

"You're bat-ass crazy." Bruce said.

Alfred reinforced Bruce's comment.

"Don't do it, Mark. Seriously. It's just plain stupid."

I heard Bruce and Al talking, but I didn't listen to a word of it. I was lost in my thoughts. I shared how I thought we should proceed.

"Get ready to video this on your phone Al. OK Mark, this is the way I think you should do this. Once Al says he's ready, step out of the car very slowly. After you are out, just stand there for a minute to see if that's enough to get it moving. If it moves even a little bit, jump back in the car. If not, take a few steps toward it, again, very slowly. Stop and see if it moves. I don't think you should cut the distance between yourself and the gator by more than half-way from where we now sit. If he comes for you, you need to be able to make it back to the car. Don't take any unnecessary chances by getting too close."

Mark was nodding his head as I spoke, although I wasn't completely sure how much he was actually hearing. He then made a sound like a pressure cooking letting off steam.

"Shhhhh... I think it'll be off to the races as soon as I open the door. One way to find out. Let's do this!"

Before Mark got out, Al gave Mark one last bit of instruction.

"Leave the keys in the car."

Mark laughed and pulled on the door latch, leaving the keys in the ignition. Alfred started the video and nodded to Mark. The game was on.

Listen reader, we've all been guilty of doing stupid things, right? That being said, I'm not sure why these four morons are constantly raising the stupid-bar for the rest of us. It's a mystery to me how they've managed to make it into their sixties.

Right on cue, Mark stepped out and closed the door behind him. He stood there without moving further. The gator remained stoic, seemingly uninterested in Mark's sudden appearance. Mark took about five large steps closer to the gator.

"You getting this Al?" I asked. He nodded in the affirmative.

Still no movement from our new friend, and now Mark wasn't moving either. He just stood there for what seemed like an eternity, but was probably only a minute. Finally, he started taking the additional steps that would bring him to about the halfway point between the car and the gator. It was here, after about Mark's third step of this round, the gator decided it had enough.

In one incredibly fast movement, the alligator swung around into a position directly facing Mark. Simultaneous with this movement was the opening of the beast's jaws, exposing fearsome teeth while releasing a horrible, dinosaur-like sound. From inside the car, we were all gasping. Mark matched the gator's speed, spinning around to face the car and started to run. Two steps into his sprint, he lost his footing on the damp grass and fell on his face. Alfred leaned over and opened the driver's door as we all yelled for Mark to hurry and get up, as if he needed more encouragement! In one synchronized motion, the other three doors popped open just in case we needed to distract the beast long enough for Mark to recover. But Mark was back on his feet in a flash and continued his short run at full speed. Everyone in the car continued yelling, but nobody was listening. I momentarily looked over in Al's direction and noticed that despite his and everyone else's yelling, he was keeping the iPhone on target.

Luckily for Mark, the gator had apparently decided that the scare it put into this human was enough. Maybe it felt sorry for a creature that was so dumb and so clumsy, or maybe it was just laughing (do gators laugh?) too hard at the sight of Mark lying face down in the wet grass. Whatever the reason, we all breathed a sigh of relief when Mark jumped in the car and slammed the door. The other three doors quickly followed suit. Mark was understandably breathing heavily and his face was even more pale than normal.

"Did you guys see that shit? Did you see how fast it

was?"

In another example of bad judgment, I reminded Mark that I said the gator was PROBABLY slow, with emphasis on the word probably.

"Well, I'm PROBABLY going to kill you after I catch my breath Schumacher!"

Now to be clear, Mark could have very easily been killed by that gator. This plan quickly devolved into a serious near-death situation. So why is it, at that exact moment, we all began laughing our fool heads off... including Mark? Just the whole stupid idea of it, and the fact that Mark was actually willing to do it, was too much for us. Part of my laughter was camouflaged relief, since I had blessed the crazy plan in the first place.

It was Alfred who broke the laughter when he yelled out "Oh shit! I didn't have the video turned on like I thought. We're going to need to do it again."

Three mouths dropped open in disbelief. For Mark, though, it was more than he could take. "I'm going to kill you, you stupid son of a bitch!"

Ha! Mark would have had better luck with the gator than with Alfred!

Alfred resumed his laughter, and while trying to catch his breath, he confessed.

"Nah man, I'm just messing with you. I got the

whole thing!"

Sighs of relieve all around. We regained our composure before continuing the journey.

To add insult to injury, the gator had wandered off without any of us even noticing. Sometime between Mark's fall and our ensuing laughter following his successful retreat, our four-legged friend with very large teeth, had apparently lost interest in us. It was OK. We captured the most important action scene. The one that would win us the Davis Avenue Award for the most bone-headed (and funniest) video of the century!

Al was about to play back the video, but I stopped him. "No Al, let's wait."

We discussed the best time to watch the video and agreed it was not while we were in the car. We needed to get moving again if we were going to make it on time for our African Queen adventure. We decided we wouldn't watch it until after we finished our cruise, and when we were back in one of the hotel rooms. It would be a tough wait, but it would also be worth it.

Alfred couldn't resist one last jab.

"Hey Mark, should we stop somewhere? You know… in case you need to do some house cleaning in your drawers!"

For perhaps the first time in his life, Mark had no response.

We settled down and continued south toward Key

Largo. It seemed like only minutes before the Taurus was rolling along on the Overseas Highway, which connects the Florida mainland to Key Largo and then onward all the way to Key West. Our short Everglades adventure was over, but would certainly remain legendary for years to come! For now, however, Key Largo would soon become our one-night resting place. We had a date with a queen.

10 – THE QUEEN

We rolled into Key Largo with little time to spare. Due to our unexpected encounter with grumpy-gator, we pulled into the hotel parking lot at 3:40pm. That left us 20 minutes to check-in, drop our bags off in the rooms, and immediately run out to make our 4pm reservation on the African Queen. Luckily for us, Bruce had masterfully arranged for rooms at the Holiday Inn that was adjacent to the Queen's berth on a canal. We stepped outside, and there she was... the African Queen. Bruce noticed Alfred was carrying something wrapped in a brown paper bag, and asked him what he had. To me, it looked suspiciously like it might contain a bottle of liquor. Al would only say it was a surprise for later. There was no time for debate. We were all engrossed with the vision before us.

As befitting a truly regal lady, a tarp was suspended

with poles above the Queen to protect her from the sun and the elements. The first thing that popped out for us was the prominent boiler located near the center of the boat. This is the boiler that gave Charlie Allnut (Humphrey Bogart), so many problems throughout the movie. He would constantly have to kick it to keep it running. We were awe struck. Each of us had our iPhones in-hand, clicking dozens of pictures. We met the captain who introduced himself, and invited us to step aboard the floating legend. I can't remember the captain's name.

No surprise there. Schumacher has never been very good at remembering people's names. The captain's name is Dave. Now how hard is that? Jeez, Dude!

"This is unbelievable" I said as we all walked around the small perimeter of the boat.

The boiler, the rudder, the life preservers, the oil lamp, the ropes, the wooden crate with Gordon's Gin painted on its side, the British Union Jack – no detail was minor or overlooked. Each was iconic for us, and revived memories of our childhood weekends in front of the TV hoping Charlie and Rosie would somehow survive. If we did nothing other than stand on the deck of that boat, we would have been completely satisfied and thrilled. But the captain had much more in store for us. I sure wish I could remember his name.

You can't see it, but my eyes are rolling right now.

With introductions and niceties out of the way, the captain flashed a big smile, clapped his hands with enthusiasm, and said "Are you guys ready to start cruising?"

"Absolutely," shouted Alfred.

"We can't wait," exclaimed Bruce. Mark agreed, "Yeah, let's shove off!"

With that, the engine started, the Queen was unmoored from the dock, and we slowly pulled out into the canal. The captain... I want to say his name was Bill...

Nope!

...began the cruise by offering several facts and trivia about the boat and the movie as we moved through the canal. Some of what he said, we already knew. For instance, the fact that Humphrey Bogart won the Academy Award for Best Actor for his performance in the movie, was well known by each of us. We also knew that Director John Huston thought Hepburn was originally playing the role of Rosie a bit too rigid, and suggested that she consider playing the role more in the mold of Eleanor Roosevelt. Hepburn later credited Huston for that excellent piece of direction. But we also learned many new tidbits related to the movie and the cast, such as the fact that the African Queen began its life as the L.S. Livingston. It was built in 1912, and was used by the British East India Company to shuttle passengers and cargo across Lake Albert between Uganda and the Belgian Congo. Also, it is actually propelled by a diesel engine, not the boiler, which was added as a prop for the movie. He told us how everyone in the cast and the crew got sick during the filming in Africa, with the exception of Humphrey Bogart and John Huston. These two supposedly avoided sickness by drinking only whiskey and eating only canned goods. This excessive drinking of alcohol apparently upset Katharine Hepburn, who in protest, drank only water during the filming. This led to her having a severe case of dysentery. At one point, she had to run to an outhouse, but upon arrival found a deadly black mamba snake inside. She then ran to some trees for relief. The captain… maybe it was Bob…

Nope!

… told us that Lauren Bacall, who was married to Bogart, accompanied him to Africa, where she and Kate Hepburn struck up what was to become a lifelong friendship.

We slowly trolled along the canal, seeing some grand homes on the banks, as well as more modest homes that were brightly painted in pastel colors. It was at this point, about a half hour into our 90-minute cruise, that Al broke out his surprise. It was a bottle of Gordon's Gin, in memory of Mr. Allnut's favorite beverage in the movie, much to Rosie's chagrin. The captain... Wait... it was DAVE... That's it! Captain Dave gave us the nod, indicating that it was OK for us to toast the Queen. Each of us took a swig, or two, or three, from the bottle. It was a perfect tribute!

He finally got the name right. Well even a broken clock is right twice a day.

After the toasting was completed, Captain Dave asked if any of us wanted to take the rudder for a while. There were definitely no dissenting voices to that question. Now I should take a second here, and wonder aloud if it was good judgment to give four morons control of the boat immediately after they had just sucked down a half bottle of gin. At the time, it seemed like a great idea to the four of us. In retrospect, however, I have to question the wisdom of Captain Dave's offer.

In the movie, Rosie successfully navigated the Queen down wild rapids, while Charlie kept the engine from failing. We figured if Rosie could do that, we could certainly do the same on this calm canal. With this logic firmly planted, we each took our turn at the rudder.

Bruce was first. What I remember most about his turn, wasn't how well he steered the boat. I guess he did fine in that regard since we're all still alive. No, what I remember most is how he pelted Captain Dave with his incessant comments and questions.

"What is the top speed of this boat?"

"How wide is the beam?"

"What is the Queen's displacement?"

"How deep does it draft?"

I just had to turn my head and laugh a little as Captain Dave played Trivial Pursuit with Bruce.

I was next. I was surprised how responsive the boat was… how easy it was to control. The hardest part was that I didn't know any of the rules regarding boating. I didn't know what the different signs and buoys meant, and I didn't know if there were rules regarding passing boats traveling in our direction or in the opposite direction. Luckily, Captain Dave was right there to make sure I didn't do anything too stupid. That role… doing something stupid… fell to Al and Mark.

Al took the rudder after me. He is by nature, balanced and calm, and this would serve him well as he steered the boat. On the other hand, he can also be prone to lack of focus, a trait less desired for a helmsman. He was so excited to be there, to be steering the actual

African Queen, that he wanted to capture himself in the moment with multiple selfies on his cell phone. Captain Dave had momentarily turned his head to respond to one of Bruce's questions that required a more complex response at the exact moment Al started clicking pictures of himself for posterity. The African Queen began straying into the path of an oncoming yacht. The yacht sounded its horn and took what little evasive measure it could take given the narrow canal. Needless to say, this got Captain Dave's attention. He quickly reached for the rudder and corrected our course as the rest of us watched wide-eyed. Alfred apologized multiple times for his indiscretion, and Captain Dave was very gracious, indicating it was fine and this sort of thing was not uncommon.

When Al gave up the rudder to Mark, he came and sat down next to me. I was less gracious, laughing at him and ribbing him about his sub-par performance. He knew he deserved it and took it well while implying it was worth it as he showed me his pictures, which would no doubt be accompanied by a highly edited version of the story when he showed them to others in the future.

Mark started off fine. He was bound and determined to show Al how much better he was as the Queen's new master and commander. Being the last to take control, it was Mark who had the honor of bringing the Queen into the Atlantic Ocean as she departed the canal. The tour did not include an extensive experience on the ocean. Captain Dave just wanted us to briefly see it and then turn around to start heading back to the dock. The ocean was choppy, causing the Queen to rise and fall. We were all glad that we would not have to endure that for long.

Captain Dave told Mark that he wanted us to turn around after we passed another large yacht that was entering the canal. He said he would let Mark know when to make the turn. This was the part of the instructions that Mark disputes.

Mark's side of the story was and is that he never heard Captain Dave indicate that he would let Mark know when to make the turn. He swears to this day that the only instructions were to turn the boat around after the yacht passed, and head to the dock. Being the type of person, whose patience has never been a strength, Mark pushed hard on the rudder within seconds of the yacht passing us. The African Queen violently swung into action. She leaned hard to the left (also known as the Port side of the ship), hitting the recently passed yacht's fairly significant wake at an awkward angle. We rose high in the water and came down hard, taking on a bit of water at the Queen's bow. Captain Dave yelled some obscenity, it doesn't matter which one, and quickly wrested control of the boat from Mark's clearly unreliable hands.

Captain Dave regained control of the boat, as well as

his emotions. He flashed everyone a smile and assured us that everything was once again fine.

"No problem at all, fellas! It would have been much smoother if we waited another minute before making our turn, and perhaps turning more gradually, but that's OK. This is how we learn. Good job everyone!"

This guy was obviously a professional, both in terms of his seamanship, and his customer relationship skills.

The rest of us, however, never really honed those skills. But we certainly could spot a weakness when one presented itself. It was an opportunity that none of us could resist.

"Nice going Captain Crunch! You nearly sunk one of the most famous boats in movie making history," I said.

"If you're going to drive a car with the same aggression that you drive the Queen, I'd just assume you not drive the car back to Staten Island," added Alfred. "You obviously can't be trusted."

Bruce just said, "What the fuck, man. I thought getting out of the car with the gator this morning would be the dumbest thing you'd do today. I stand corrected!"

Mark was obviously embarrassed (as he should have been), but it would have been out of character for him to respond with any form of repentance. Instead, he looked at us like we were the crazy ones while launching his expected defense.

"Can you ladies please stop your crying? If you need your tissues, I'm sure you have them tucked away neatly in your purses. I just showed all of you how to execute a successful power-turn under less-than-ideal conditions, and now your jealousy is flaring up almost as much as your herpes."

That was a good one, so we had to reward him with a round of well-deserved laughter. We would, however, remind Mark of this event at every conceivable opportunity down the road. He would expect nothing less from us.

Captain Dave brought us (safely) back to the dock, and our African Queen adventure was completed. It was everything we thought it would be, and quite a bit more. We departed the boat, thanked Captain Dave, and walked back to the hotel. It was time to watch the video of Mark's close encounter of the gator-kind! What a day this turned out to be. I was privately hoping that we could finish this trip with an occasional boring day thrown in here and there. Lunacy can be exhausting.

✳

We decided to watch the video in the room that Bruce and Mark were sharing. Originally, we thought we would just gather around and watch it on Al's iPhone, but we were lucky enough to have a TV in the room that was Apple AirPlay 2 compatible. (I didn't know what that meant either until Al explained it). This allowed us to stream directly from the iPhone to the TV so we could watch the video on a grand scale.

After a few false starts due to technical difficulties (Al's way of describing user error), Al was ready to start the show.

"Are you ready for the action, boys?"

"You bet! Fire it up Al!" Mark responded.

The video only lasted three or four minutes but it was off-the-charts funny! If you combined the funniest three movies you ever saw in your life into one super-movie, you wouldn't even get close to the laugh value of this video. With only a few brief exceptions, Al kept the camera steady as he recorded the action. He had a perfect angle from the car and flawlessly captured the gator's lightning turn and display of its mouthful of sharp teeth. As Mark spun to retreat, the look of horror on his bright red face was pricelessly captured in living color. The only time Al momentarily lost the subjects from the video was when Mark fell. That was when Al and the rest of us were opening the car doors, preparing for the worst. But he quickly recovered, and we could see Mark's terror as he rose and ran to the car. Al also caught something quite by accident.

After Mark was back in the car, and while everyone was still screaming, Al's iPhone was facing in the general direction of the gator without our cameraman even realizing it. For the first time we saw the beast slowly turn away from us and head back into the brush.

I don't know how many times we watched that video that evening, but it had to be at least a dozen times. I had a sore throat from laughing so hard, and I'm sure I was not alone with that symptom.

I did the best I could to explain to you how funny that video is, but it's really impossible for me to do it the justice it deserves. The only thing I can say is this. If you ever see Alfred on the street somewhere, ask him to let you watch it. I promise, you won't be sorry.

We decided that we would take it easy for the rest of the day. I think we earned the rest. So, we just wandered around the waterfront near the hotel for an hour or so. We looked in a bunch of shops (didn't buy anything), and we found a small restaurant that had a bar. It was a bit early for dinner, but we got two orders of nachos to share, and tried out some local beers. By the time we left that place, nobody felt like eating anything else, so we just went back to the hotel and decided to make it an early night. The final leg of our journey prior to returning to Staten Island lay before us

11 – DAY SIX

October 19th

Mark wanted to be the one to drive into Key West. We were happy to confer that honor to him, although not before bestowing on him a few quick references to his questionable skills at operating motor-powered vehicles... especially boats. He uncharacteristically ignored these veiled attempts to get his goat. He must have been tired. The prior day took a lot out of us, although none of us would ever admit that.

Willie Nelson and Waylon Jennings penned a song several years ago called 'Old Age and Treachery' where they sang about how they could still jump as high... (referring to their Get-Up-And-Go) ... but they just couldn't stay that high that long (referring to their lack of stamina). It happens to the best of us!

We once again took advantage of the free breakfast

at the hotel. Afterward, Bruce and Al went back to the rooms to collect their luggage. This gave me the opportunity I was looking for to talk with Mark in private. As we finished our coffees, I reminded him of our agreement.

"Don't forget, dude, you promised that you would spill the beans about your planned engagement when we got to Key West. That's today!"

"Yeah, yeah, I know. Sometime while we're in Key West, I'll tell them."

"Oh no you don't," I said. "You're going to tell them today, and if you don't, I will. I'm not keeping this secret for you any longer."

"OK, man, chill out. I'll tell them today after we arrive. How about while we're at lunch?"

"Yeah, that's fine."

"OK deal. But make sure you don't let on that you already know. I don't want either of their feminine feelings hurt."

With business concluded, Mark and I followed the others up to the rooms, collected our luggage, and checked out.

We were rolling by 9:30am. Key West was 107 miles away – just over a two-hour drive without stops according to the GPS. Our long-awaited, and much-anticipated final destination was well within sight.

The drive along the Overseas Highway was

fascinating. For portions of the trip, we could see the Atlantic Ocean on one side of the car, and the Gulf of Mexico on the other, broken only by stretches of small towns on the various islands. Bruce googled the Florida Keys on his phone while we drove, and read to us some of the interesting facts about the chain. We learned that the Keys are made up of over 1700 islands, islets (very small, often unnamed islands), and cays (a small, low island, situated on a coral reef), but the main ones are Key Largo, Islamorada, Marathon, Big Pine Key, and Key West.

Throughout our trip, we had been noticing the warmer temperatures. By the time we got to South Carolina and beyond, the difference in temperatures became more dramatic. When we left Staten Island, the temperatures peaked in the mid fifty-degree range. Now, as we approached Key West, they were hitting the low to mid-eighties. Of course, none of us brought any shorts to wear… primarily because none of us own a pair of shorts. As young children, our parents dressed us in shorts, but that tradition died around the time we reached our pre-teen years. Each of us did, however, pack a swim suit, although the odds of them seeing the light of day on this trip were low. We had jeans and T-shirts… didn't really need anything else.

As we passed through the various islands, I thought to myself that it would be great to return someday and spend some time in each. I'm not a fisherman or a sportsman, by any stretch of the imagination, but I loved the view of the ocean, the warm sun, and the great variety of restaurants and small bars that each location seemed to offer. I do hope to return. Someday.

The gray Taurus, loaded with four wide-eyed New Yorkers, rolled onto Key West at 11:48am on October 19th. It reminded me of when we were on the bridge leaving Staten Island. The same silence in the car. I guess silence is an appropriate response to any life milestone, and this certainly felt like that.

Key West was exactly as I had pictured it. Palm trees, small wood frame homes surrounded with colorful tropical flowers, and of course, the sky-blue ocean. It was teeming with people, most of whom were either walking or riding bicycles. As we approached our motel on Duval Street, we were surrounded by all sorts of restaurants and bars – more than I could count. We even passed a red brick building with a sign that read 'Better Than Sex.' I tucked that away in the back of my head. We'll have to find out what that is.

I'm not sure if, and when, we'll get back to this, so I better clarify here. 'Better Than Sex' is the name of a restaurant that is only open at night. They sell outrageous desserts and sweet mixed drinks. What were you thinking??

Duval Street itself was clearly the hot spot. It was wall-to-wall bars, restaurants, touristy shops, and night clubs. We could probably spend two weeks just walking up and down this one street, and still not have seen everything. Our excitement was building as we viewed this tropical circus. We pulled into our motel, which was exactly as Bruce described it. An old-style motel that, other than its mid-century modern styling, looked brand new. It had a pool, and the rooms themselves were small but nice. For Key West, Mark and I bunked together, with Al and Bruce in the adjoining room. We quickly unpacked, splashed some water on our faces and headed out. Of course, not before I gave Mark one more reminder.

He thanked me in his own way.

"Enough Dick-Wad! I'll tell them!"

I smiled. "OK, grab four celebratory cigars. We'll find a place to smoke them after you make your announcement."

*

The first part of our Key West expedition would be a walk along Duval Street. We were ready for lunch and certainly had our choice of cuisines. I insisted on a fish restaurant of some sort, since I was craving some fresh shrimp. That was an easy choice for the group. There was so much to see on Duval. I was surprised by the diverse nature of the street. Art galleries and antique stores, intertwined with souvenir T-shirt shops and drag-show bars. The dichotomy between traditional art, culture, and architecture, interspersed with the gaudy and the outrageous, was astounding. It seemed to combine the heartbeat and the libido of Key West to create one marvelous mixed salad of humanity. The sidewalks were crammed with people, and I wondered if this was normal for this time of year or if it was due to the upcoming Fantasy Fest events. Regardless, the energy was palpable, and I was thrilled that we were there to participate. I could tell my friends were equally energized.

We came upon a seafood place called Pinchers Crab Shack, located on the second floor of an intricately decorated wooden building above some shops. It looked like a perfect place to order shrimp and get some drinks, so we went in. The first thing a customer sees upon entering is a fish tank with live lobsters, beyond which was a large crowded bar leading to a covered outdoor deck. We had chosen wisely. The hostess brought us to a table along the railing of the deck. From here we would be able to enjoy our lunch while people-watching those strolling down Duval, all at the same time.

Much like the restaurant itself, the menu was exactly

what we were looking for. A wide variety of seafood as well as burgers, ribs, pasta and a dozen different types of sandwiches. The waitress taking our order was an attractive young lady named Alina from Bucharest, Romania. Although she had a slight accent, her English was near perfect and she was very friendly. It seems we liked everything about this place.

I ordered the Coconut Shrimp with Conch Fritters and chased it with a Rum Runner mixed drink. Al ordered the same, except he ordered a beer. Mark got Pasta Shrimp Scampi with a beer and Bruce ordered some kind of humongous burger with fries and a Jameson whiskey.

With that out of the way, I waited… impatiently… for Mark to speak up. At first, he was quiet and, I believe, intentionally avoiding eye contact with me. That was understandable given the circumstances, but I would only give him so much leeway. The food and drinks were delivered to our table. After a few sips of liquid courage, he finally spoke up.

"Hey, guys, I've got something I want to tell you. It's a big deal."

"What's the matter, Mark?" Alfred could tell by Mark's expression and his tone that this was important. He, and the others, were clearly concerned. I, on the other hand, was relieved, although I did my best to not let that show.

Mark then launched into what was pretty much the same speech he recited to me back in Delaware. He told us he was going to propose to someone he'd been seeing, he told them her name, where and when they met, where she lived and worked... the whole spiel. Nobody interrupted, but when he paused, he was hit with a barrage of questions.

Their reaction was similar to my own. Shock and disbelief summed it up the best. At one point, Bruce almost blew my cover when he asked me why I was being so quiet about all of this. I had to think quickly since I didn't anticipate questions directed at me.

"I just don't know what to say. I can't believe what I'm hearing, but I'm happy for you, Mark."

The others quick seconded that congratulatory remark before resuming their inquisition. It was Alfred who asked the one question the rest of us failed to ask.

"Where are you going to live? You're not leaving Davis Avenue, are you?"

"No way!" Mark waved his hands, and shook his head vehemently. "You guys don't have to worry about that at all. Isabel only rents a place, so if she says she will marry me, we will live in my house. I'll never break up the gang. This doesn't change us."

I felt a strong need to speak up. "Well, Mark, it won't just be your decision. She'll have a say in this, too."

"Yes, of course. I know that. But I also know her,

and she will understand. I've told her all about you guys, including that we've lived as neighbors for our whole lives. She told me she was so glad that I had such close, and longtime friends, and she hoped it would last forever."

Then, as an afterthought, he added,

"Oh, and by the way, you guys don't have to worry. I lied my ass off to her to make each of you look like normal, decent humans."

With a smile Bruce told Mark what the rest of us were thinking.

"We appreciate you lying about us, Mark, and I hope you're right about her agreeing to live on Davis Avenue. I'd hate to have to stand up at the part of the ceremony where they say – If anyone has a reason why this couple should not get married – blah, blah, blah… because I sure as hell won't hold my peace."

Mark laughed. "Fair enough, Bruce. Fair enough."

Al had the last question. Well, the last question for now.

"When are you planning to pop the question?"

There was no hesitation in Mark's response.

"As soon as I can, after we get back from this trip. I was thinking about giving her my mother's engagement ring. Do you think that's OK, John?"

"Hmmmm. Well, I guess so. It seems like a nice idea… a connection between your past life and your new one… but you might also want to ask that question to a woman. A female might have a different perspective on that. I'm just not sure."

"Yeah, good idea, John, I'll ask a woman. So, Bruce, what do you think?"

We all broke up at that, and were grateful for the levity.

I knew from my discussion with Mark in Delaware, that this was a lot for Al and Bruce to absorb. I was sure there would be many more questions, but I was equally sure that this moment went very well, and that they were both as happy for Mark as I was.

We took our time at the restaurant and had two drink refills each as we sat there enjoying each other's company, and watching the masses from our perch above Duval Street. After a while though, we all started feeling the urge to do more exploring. Mark told everyone he had the four Cohibas (the cigars I secretly suggested he bring along).

"Let's find a place to light them up and continue celebrating!"

This suggestion was approved without dissent.

*

We ended up at Mallory Square. We were told by a street vendor that it would be a good place to smoke cigars, and as a bonus it was a great place to watch the sunset. Mallory Square sits on the waterfront, giving spectators amazing views of the sun as it slowly dips below the horizon. It was a fairly short walk, as are most places in Key West. We passed Sloppy Joe's, which was Ernest Hemingway's favorite hang-out, and now an iconic landmark. Another historic site, the Hemingway House, was nearby but it's basically a museum, so we decided to just stick with Sloppy Joe's on our "must do" list. We also passed a bar that looked like our kind of place called Hog's Breath Saloon. We put that one on our list as well.

Mallory Square was a great location to enjoy the cigars. We were able to sit on the seawall, and the cigar smoke ensured that we wouldn't have a bunch of people around to bother us. Sunset was still a couple of hours away, but the cigars would burn for an hour, and there seemed to be plenty to do around Mallory Square while we waited. The longer we sat there, the more the square started filling up. Vendors of all types… jewelry, art, food… started setting up. Street performers, such as jugglers, dancers, and musicians began to ply their trades. After we finished our cigars, we killed some time by taking advantage of these activities. I noticed Mark bought a necklace made from pieces of old glass wine bottles. I didn't have to ask who the gift was for, and I was certain that Isabel would like his choice.

As we continued to explore, we walked by a Cuban

restaurant that bordered Mallory Square called El Mason de Pepe. They had a menu displayed and what caught my eye was the prominently displayed Cuban Sandwich.

"Hey, guys, look at this. They have Cuban Sandwiches. Let's eat here after the sunset."

"Sounds good to me," Bruce said. "Especially since you were looking forward to having one in Miami, which I derailed with my suggestion to skip Miami and replace it with Key Largo."

"Thanks, Bruce, but you were definitely right about bypassing Miami for Key Largo. Even though Mark tried to kill us and sink the African Queen with one brainless maneuver."

Three laughs… One middle finger.

I could tell there was no need for additional voting, so we went over to the hostess and reserved a table for 7PM, just after the sunset.

In case you live on Mars, dear reader, a Cuban Sandwich is roast pork with ham, Swiss cheese, pickles, and yellow mustard. It's all layered on a crusty Cuban roll, and the whole thing is heated to perfection in a press. It is a heavenly creation.

We returned to the seawall, along with a couple thousand of our closest friends, and watched the sun set into the sea. I have to admit, even though I've seen beautiful sunsets in the past, this one in Key West was truly spectacular. The fact that the four of us watched it together in silence made it all the more special. It is a local custom for onlookers to clap as the sun touches the horizon, and it was truly applause worthy.

Now… time for those sandwiches and a large slice of Key Lime Pie! What a way to top off the evening. After gorging ourselves to the point of the predictable meat-sweats, we all decided to head back to the motel and make it an early night. It was a big day of travel and adventure, and we needed our rest. As sixty-somethings, we've learned to pace ourselves.

12 – DAY SEVEN

October 20th

The next morning, we asked a gentleman at the front desk where there was a good place to have breakfast. He told us there were probably twenty good places within a short walk of our location, but he said his personal favorite was Blue Heaven. He gave us the directions, and off we went.

The restaurant was something that you would only see in Key West. Even though they had indoor dining, almost everyone, including us, chose to eat outside. It was a spacious, fenced area shaded with large trees and colorful tarps. What struck us most, however, were the free roaming roosters and hens. It was an unusual site, but we loved it. There are chickens wandering all over Key West, but I wasn't expecting to see them where we were eating. The locals love and protect their funky fowls, while the chickens themselves have become accustomed to sharing their spaces with all of the strange humans. Roosters are so popular that they have become the unofficial mascot of Key West. Once again, this trip surprises us at nearly every turn.

The menu ran the gamut with all types of amazing breakfast foods, but the one thing that caught our eyes was the pancake selection. For years, whenever the four of us went out to eat breakfast, we would all end up ordering pancakes. One more thing we had in common with each other was the love for these tasty desserts disguised as a breakfast. Alfred and I leaned toward the pecan variety, while Bruce and Mark preferred blueberries. We all stuck with our favorites, adding bacon, sausage, and a couple of pots of black coffee. We were not disappointed. Toward the end of our meal, I did my daily itinerary check with my fellow travelers.

"OK, boys. What's the agenda for today? I know we all wanted to go to Sloppy Joe's today, and I'd suggest we eat dinner there. I checked online and they have a good selection of bar food like wings, nachos, pizza, and a bunch of other stuff. I have a suggestion for the rest of the day, but I'm wondering what you guys want to do."

Al spoke up first.

"I'm open to suggestions, too. I did hear about a bar that's supposed to be very popular called The Green Parrot. But I don't think we should go there the same day we go to Sloppy Joe's. Maybe tomorrow?"

Mark agreed with Al and suggested we save that for

another night. He then pushed back on me.

"C'mon John, just give us your suggestion. If we don't like it, we won't be shy about shooting it down. You should know that."

"OK, I just didn't want to come off as the agenda Nazi. My thought is we go to the beach. Zachary Taylor Beach is really close and it's a public beach in a State Park."

Bruce wasn't thrilled (NOT!)

"A beach? Really?"

I nodded to show him that I understood his skepticism, but explained further.

"Look, I know we aren't exactly beach bums, but this is Key West after all. We should go at least once on this trip. I heard this beach has trees where we can stay out of the sun if it gets too hot. Plus, they have a place that sells food and beer."

"I have a better idea," said Bruce. "Let's stop at a liquor store... I saw one on Duval... and fill up some water bottles with our own drinks. I really don't want to spend a fortune for a beer."

"That sounds good to me," I said.

"OK then," Al said. "It's settled. We'll go to the beach after picking up some liquor and filling the water bottles."

"I don't have one," said Mark, "...but I can pick up a cheap water bottle in one of those T-shirt stores. So, the beach it is, but I like the idea of staying in the shade. We can drink while we stare at the ocean. I'm sure not going swimming."

Everyone was on the same page about not swimming. This is just one of those activities that people do on vacation that just checks a box. That way, when someone says, "Oh I was there a year ago, and wasn't the beach beautiful?" we can say, "Yep, it sure was!" Besides, how bad can it be to sit on a shady beach while enjoying our favorite beverages and good cigars?

Al had a good energy-saving idea to add.

"Let's rent bikes for a few of days. We can ride down to the beach and bring those beach chairs that the motel lends out. They have straps so we can carry them like backpacks. The bikes even have baskets for our drinks and towels."

"Perfect, Al" I said. "Good idea."

We paid our breakfast bills and walked to the nearest bike rental place. From there we rode to the liquor store where we stocked up, then to a T-shirt place where Mark picked up a water bottle, and eventually back to the motel to get ready for our beach trip.

$$*$$

Within the hour, we had pulled everything together and arrived at Fort Zachary Taylor State Park. We each paid our $2.50 entrance fee, locked up our bikes in a rack, and found a great spot to sit. It was a different kind of beach than what we were used to on Staten Island. The beaches there, such as Midland Beach or South Beach were wide sandy beaches, similar to what we saw on this trip, although not as wide as Daytona. This beach was made up of a mixture of sand and small pebbles with a few large rocky outcrops. Lining the beach were thick groupings of trees. We decided to settle where the trees and the beach collided. The tree-line would give us the shade we desired, while also having an unobstructed view of the ocean about twenty-five yards away. It was perfect for city boys who were mostly interested in avoiding the ubiquitous sun while enjoying our drinks with a good view. Our jeans, sneakers, and t-shirts pretty much dictated that we would avoid the sun as much as possible.

Oh brother. These guys are embarrassing. Of course, they did everyone else a favor by not overly exposing their bright white sixty-something bodies.

We were there for about thirty-minutes, enjoying the view, and making up lies about each other, when I spotted something. About one hundred and fifty yards off-shore, four small motorboats sat motionless. The boats were separated from each other by about thirty yards in a line parallel to the beach. Dispersed in the water not far from the boats, were small rounded objects. They were too far away for me to see clearly, but I thought they were either heads or buoys bobbing around. I pointed this out to the others.

"Hey guys, check out those boats. Can any of you make out what's in the water next to them? Are they heads or buoys or what?"

Al thought they were heads.

"Maybe they're taking diving lessons or snorkeling."

Mark disagreed.

"I don't think so, Al. I think they're too big for heads. I'm gonna go with buoys that are being used to warn other boats that there are divers in the water or something like that."

Bruce agreed with Mark.

"Yeah, Mark. Definitely too big to be heads."

We didn't think too much of it at first, and I only watched intermittently between swigs of my drink. I was trying to keep up with the others. But I did start to notice a change.

"Dudes, those buoys or whatever they are, are getting closer. They were definitely further away ten-minutes ago."

Bruce pointed out something else.

"Yes, and the boats are a little closer, too. So that means that the buoys, if that is what they are, aren't anchored. If there are divers down there, they must be tethered to the buoys, and are now headed for the beach."

There were other people on the beach, but they all seemed oblivious to the approach of the mystery buoys. Myself and my comrades, however, were now laser-focused on this activity.

It was around this time that Al noticed the chain link fence that was to our left as we faced the ocean. It was about thirty or forty yards from where we set up our chairs. It didn't even register with us previously, but it was now interesting for two reasons. First of all, the fence was topped with barbed wire. (How did I not notice that before?) It separated the beach into two parts and it didn't stop at the waterline. It extended thirty or forty fee beyond that point, well into the water. Secondly, if the supposed buoys maintained their current course, some would come in directly in front of us, but most would come ashore on the other side of the fence.

So, we just waited, assuming that this mystery would soon resolve itself given the movement of the buoys. It was clear now that the bobbing objects were not heads, but indeed small buoys, about twice the size of a football. They were now only about twenty yards from the shoreline.

And then it happened. At first, we saw men's heads and shoulders in the water. They were not wearing diving masks. This wasn't a scuba or snorkeling class.

As they made their way into more shallow water, we saw that these guys were carrying assault rifles and fully decked out in some type of military garb. They didn't have typical oxygen tanks like you would see being used by recreational or commercial divers. They were wearing some strange looking backpacks, which must have contained some type of breathing apparatus since these men were underwater for a long time.

We were obviously shocked to be seeing this.

"What the fuck is this all about?" Al said.

I responded.

"I have no idea, but we should get out of these chairs just in case. I'm going to take some picture with my cell phone."

"I'll do the same, but first let's move back behind some trees," said Al.

Bruce made a good observation.

"These guys aren't looking at us, and don't seem to care less what we're doing here. They're just pulling in those buoys, and heading over to the fence with the barbed wire. This must be some kind of military training."

That ended up being exactly the case. We didn't realize this, but the property on the other side of the fence was a military installation. We also didn't know that the U.S. Army maintains a Special Forces facility on a small island adjacent to Key West. Although we can't know this for certain, we speculated that all of the soldiers were supposed to come ashore on the military side of the fence. Most did, but there were a few who came in directly in front of where we were lounging and starting to feel buzzed from our drinks.

The few that came in on our side of the fence, took what I will call the long and slow walk-of-shame, making their way around the fence to meet up with their comrades. We were able to get some good photos of this incursion after realizing we probably weren't going to be killed in action. About a half hour after they first emerged from the water, our invaders were nowhere to be seen. We sat back down on our chairs and resumed drinking. We swallowed more vigorously than the sips we took prior to the commencement of World War III.

✳

When we got back to the motel, we decided to combine the four chairs sitting outside our rooms so we could contemplate the day. It was a nice place to sit and relax since it was covered with a portico and faced the pool. It would have been a perfect place for a cigar, but smoking was prohibited anywhere on the motel grounds. We were, however, able to refill our water bottles… not with water.

"I'm going to have to stop hanging around with you

guys," I said. "A guy of my vintage can only take so much excitement."

Mark was quickest with his denunciation.

"This whole trip was your idea, Schumacher. I don't want to hear your crap about being overly excited!"

"And more specifically..." added Alfred "...it was you who recommended the beach today."

Bruce took the last shot.

"Uh huh... And you didn't say anything about the beach being ground-zero for a new D-Day invasion. That piece of information would have allowed us to make a more informed decision about whether we should go or not."

"Well, at least we now have a great story to tell, rather than boring our co-workers with how we went to the beach, stared at the water, and then went back to the motel." I paused, and then added, "So, you're welcome!"

"Well, I for one can really use a boring day," said Bruce.

"Speaking of boring days," I said "let's talk about your wedding, Mark."

Mark aimed his middle finger at me, and said "Sure. Shoot."

"Well, I was just wondering about a couple of things. First, how confident are you that she will say yes?"

"I was wondering the same thing, Mark," Al said. "Is

it bad luck to talk about it before she agrees to marry you?"

"I don't know about bad luck." Mark replied. "What I do know is that while you are correct that I haven't formally asked her, we have talked about it. Mostly in hypotheticals, but the fact that she even engaged in that type of conversation makes me think she wants to marry me."

He paused in thought, then continued.

"If I wasn't very confident, I would never have brought it up with you guys. I'm sure she loves me... and while I have to question her good judgment on that point, I'm sure I love her, too."

Mark's response was unexpected. The last time I remember him being so solemn and introspective was at his parent's funeral.

It was Bruce's turn to ask a wedding-related question that he'd been wanting to ask since Mark first broke the news.

"OK, I'm going to ask an indelicate and a presumptuous question. You've known the three of us since childhood. So, which one of us will be the Best Man?"

We all laughed, but it was a great question. Before Mark could answer, Bruce continued his interrogation.

"And if you feel I'm putting you on the spot, well tough shit. Man-up and tell us."

I'm glad Bruce asked the question. I have to admit that it also crossed my mind and I'm guessing Alfred was no different.

Mark was shaking his head and exhaling in an exasperated manner.

"All right. I guess I do have to pick one of you losers. Or do I? Since Isabel probably won't want any of you as bridesmaids, and since I'm equally disgusted by all of you… I guess I'll have to have three Best Men. So that's my decision. I want all three of you up there with me… standing as equals… three best men."

The three of us sat quietly for a few seconds with our mouths open.

"Mark, I don't know if that's allowed," I said.

"Fuck allowed!" I know I'm going to have very little to say about this wedding, but this one thing is mine. I own it. I will be the one to decide, and that's my decision."

"All right!" exclaimed Al.

"I love it!" said Bruce.

"Same here, Mark. Love it!" from me.

We stood up from our lawn chairs, and tapped our plastic, alcohol-filled, water bottles in a toast. It was like a modern-day version of The Three Musketeers with D'Artagnan crossing swords in an "All for one and one for all" moment. Well, OK… maybe it was more like something from The Big Lebowski, but regardless, it felt right. God help Mark when Isabel gets wind of this, but I'm sure this is one thing where there is no room for compromise. Mark will have his three Best Men.

We decided it was time for a quick snooze before heading over to Sloppy Joe's for the evening. After the heavy breakfast we had at Blue Heaven, none of us were interested in eating lunch. Instead, we agreed to a 5pm meet-up for an early dinner, giving us a couple of hours to recharge our batteries.

*

The four of us, like clockwork, stepped out of our rooms at 5pm to start our short walk to Sloppy Joe's. We're nothing, if not punctual. Within ten minutes, we were standing in front of what is arguably the most iconic spot in Key West.

Time for a Key West history lesson kids...

Sloppy Joe's began life on Greene Street, not far from its current location on Duval Street. The original name of that bar was the Blind Pig, owned by a Key West native named Joe Russell. Prior to leasing that bar, Russell was a charter boat captain, (and a rumrunner during prohibition) and this is how he met Ernest Hemingway who began visiting Key West during the winter months in 1928, and moved full-time to Key West in 1931. Russell eventually became Hemingway's boat pilot, and fishing companion for over twelve years. It was actually Hemingway who recommended changing the name of Russell's bar to Sloppy Joe's. It was a name that Hemingway knew from a bar that he frequented in Havana. Hemingway met his third wife, Martha Gellhorn, at Sloppy Joe's in 1936.

Following a rent dispute with his landlord in 1937, Joe Russell moved his entire business, lock, stock, and barrel in a single night to its current location at the intersection of Duval and Greene Streets. Technically, the bar never closed. Customers simply picked up their drinks, and their chairs, and anything else they could carry, and the bar service resumed at the new location. To thank his customers for their help, and their loyalty, Russell did not charge for drinks that night. Only in Key West!

We entered the packed bar. We were lucky to arrive just as some others were leaving, and we grabbed the newly vacant table. They have live music every night at Sloppy Joe's, but we arrived between performers, which was good since we would be able to hear ourselves talk. We ordered our drinks and food, and absorbed the ambiance of this historic building. We were sitting across from a table occupied by three Key West locals who could somehow see (easily) that we were tourists. They asked us where we were from, and we chatted for a while. These guys knew a little bit too much about the bar in my opinion, sharing with us that it was built in 1917. They pointed out beautiful Cuban tilework, and the large jalousie doors, all original to the building. Maybe more than we needed to know, but they were very friendly and we realized this was a common trait in Key West. Admittedly, this is a bit strange for four guys who spent their entire lives in a defensive posture around strangers... but it was nice. Different, like almost everything else we've seen on this trip, but definitely nice.

I excused myself after the drinks arrived. I told my buddies I was headed to the rest room, and would be right back. Luckily, none of them joined me because I actually wanted to go into the attached gift shop. I picked up four navy blue T-shirts (two XXL – Al & Bruce, one XL – Me, and one L – Mark). They had a small Sloppy Joe's logo above the heart on the front and the same, but much larger logo on the back. I returned to the table.

"What took you so long, and what do you have there?" Al asked.

"I stopped in the gift shop."

Mark had to say something, of course.

"Oh good. For a second there I thought you picked up something nice in the bathroom."

"Keep your day-job, Mark! I got us all Sloppy Joe's T-shirts." I pulled them out to show them. I honestly expected more trash talk from them, and that would have been fine with me since I know none of that crap is serious, but they actually expressed pleasure.

"Hey, man, I like that one!" from Bruce.

The others responded in kind, and thanked me for the gift. We hadn't bought any kind of souvenir on this trip, unless you count the cigars as a souvenir of North Carolina, and I thought we needed a tangible reminder of this trip, other than the photos and videos we had taken along the way. The unexpected response from my buddies made me feel like I made a good choice.

The rest of the evening was a blast. The food and the drinks were good, as was the live musical entertainment (a local musician who played a lot of Bob Marley, Peter Tosh, and Jimmy Buffet), but what really made the evening great was being in the company of good friends. Make no mistake, we didn't break any new ground by drinking responsibly, but that's OK. Just like when we drank at O'Leary's Pub on Staten Island, we arrived and left on foot. The only thing we put in danger was our dignity. A small price to pay.

We got back to our rooms around 2am. We were feeling good and making more noise than we probably should have on the way there. I was worried about waking other guests when we arrived. I was relieved to learn, however, that 2am was not considered late in Key West. There were still people in and around the pool having a good time. We didn't participate. We were more than ready to hit the sack, and hopefully sleep late in the morning.

13 – DAY EIGHT

October 21st

We all slept until nearly noon. This was uncharacteristic of us, especially true in our more "mature" years, but obviously we needed it. We hadn't talked about what we wanted to do for the day yet, but none of us were ready to do anything until we got some food and coffee into our bodies.

We walked slowly, and in relative silence, down Duval Street toward the end that we hadn't yet explored; the end that led to the Southernmost point of the United States. I'll call this the quiet end of Duval, if there really is such a thing. We passed fewer bars than what we found on the Mallory Square end of the street, and more shops of all types. After a few blocks, we found a place for breakfast called the Banana Café. From the street, we could see they had outdoor seating on a rooftop balcony, and on the first level they had open shutters giving that level an outdoor experience as well. The weather was perfect for outdoor dining, so we got a table.

Come to think of it, the weather had been perfect since the day we arrived. I wondered if residents ever got sick of it? I was talking with a guy who ran a cigar stand on Duval, and he told me that even though it's hot here in the summer, the prevailing tradewinds combine with constant sea breezes to subdue the summer heat. The closest thing we get to tradewinds or sea breezes on Staten Island are artificially generated from air conditioning and electric fans strategically arranged in our homes.

The food was good and plentiful. I thought to myself that before I leave Key West, I want to find a place where the food sucks. There's got to be one somewhere on the island, but we hadn't found it yet.

We were in no hurry to go anywhere after eating. The waitress had no problem keeping our coffee filled while we talked about plans for the day.

"What do you guys want to do today?" I asked. "I noticed that down by Mallory Square they have a glass bottom boat that goes out daily to see the coral reef offshore. Any interest?"

"Not me," said Mark. "The playoffs are on today and I want to watch the Yankees." He paused for a second, then added, "Besides, that's for tourists."

I laughed.

"Mark, I hate to break this to you, but we ARE tourists here."

I honestly think this took him by surprise. I could have called him just about anything else... an ass, a moron, anything... and he would have just laughed it off, and probably agreed with me. But a tourist? That was crossing a line in his mind. But I understand it. We've lived for so long watching and laughing at tourists in New York City... in their shorts, I-heart-NY T-shirts, and cameras around their necks... that we had a hard time seeing ourselves in that role. Clearly, this was not New York, and we were the ones taking pictures, albeit (thank goodness) without the shorts.

Mark considered my comment, although from his perspective it was more of an accusation.

"Well, you may be a tourist Schumacher, but I'm just here to keep you and the others out of trouble on this trip."

"Oh My God! Did you really just say that? You are here to keep US out of trouble?" I was shocked.

Al's comment indicated that he was equally astounded.

"And just how are you keeping us out of trouble? Is it by nearly killing us on the African Queen, or is it by getting us into a rumble with a very large, and irritable alligator?"

Bruce laughed at this, but then sided with Mark.

"Don't worry, Mark, I'm not interested in the glass bottom boat either. I'll watch the game with you."

I gave it one last shot.

"You guys know the Yanks are gonna to lose. They have a ton of power, but their pitching sucks. The Astros also have good power, and their pitching is much better than ours."

"I don't know anything of the kind, Schumacher. I think they're going to win, and I think you're a traitor. I'm watching the game," said Mark, "and Bruce is, too."

I threw in the towel.

"OK, that's fine. What about you, Al? Game or Boat?"

"I'll go with you on the boat, John. I don't mind playing the tourist role. Besides, I'd like to see Key West from the ocean's point of view."

After a couple of seconds, he looked back to Mark, adding,

"They are gonna lose, Bro. Nobody is sorrier than me about that, but they are. The Astros have the Bomber's number and you know it."

So, we at least had the early part of the day set. Half of us would watch the playoffs, and the other half would sail the ocean blue. We paid the check, and headed back to the hotel to get ready for our split agenda.

For those readers who don't follow baseball, the Yankees/Astros rivalry has been completely one-sided in favor of Houston. They beat the Yankees in the 2015 wild card game, and three more times in the American League Championship Series. It's very sad, and very frustrating for us pinstripe fans.

*

Alfred and I started out for our glass bottom boat adventure at around 2:30pm, while Mark and Bruce went to the 7-11 to pick up some beer and snacks to enjoy during the game.

When we got to the pier, we found out the next boat didn't leave until 4pm, so we had a little time to kill. Luckily, we were close to one of the bars we were interested in trying called Hogs Breath Saloon. Based on what we've seen, it's really a place better visited at night, which is when it really comes alive, but it was still a good place to kill some time. We both had a pint of draft and then looked around the gift shop for a while. I picked up another T-shirt for myself, a black one with a large wild hog emblazoned across the back. By that point, it was time to head back to the pier.

At 4pm, Alfred and I got our first view of Key West from off shore as our boat pulled away from the pier at the end of Duval Street. And yes, there were plenty of people with shorts onboard, snapping lot of photos. That was OK, though. We had a beautiful sunny day, and the ocean was calm. The tour was scheduled to last for about two hours. The boat had an indoor seating area that was air conditioned, but Al and I preferred to sit outside on some benches in the sun. The views alone were worth the cost of the tour.

We had some time to talk before we would arrive at the coral reef.

"Hey, Al, have you ever thought about retiring anytime soon?"

Apparently, he had, because he didn't take time to think about it before responding.

"Well, financially I can do it. I turn 65 next month, so I can get Medicare. I've been able to save a decent amount of money, and thanks to inheriting our parent's homes, the four of us either have very small mortgages, or none at all. Of course, there is also Social Security, but I'll probably hold off on that for a while. They say it's better to not collect it right away unless it's needed."

"OK, so you can retire soon, but will you?"

"I keep tossing it around in my head, but I haven't made a final decision yet. What slows me down about taking the plunge is the fear that I'll be bored. We've all been working in some form or fashion since we were about 14 or 15 years old. To suddenly go cold turkey is kind of scary. What about you?"

I thought about what he said, and was surprised about how closely our two perspectives paralleled each other. I guess I shouldn't have been surprised.

"What you said is exactly what I've been thinking as well. As you know, I recently started Medicare, so I'm a few months ahead of you on that point. Otherwise, it sounds like our thoughts, and our situations are the same."

Al nodded, but didn't say anything, so I decided to continue.

"I think that I'm going to do it soon though. Working at Con Ed has been great, and yes, I would miss working there. Mostly because I like the people. The job itself, however, I don't think I would miss that much at this point. I'm 65 and I don't want to be one of those people who dies before having a chance to enjoy retirement. I'm right on the edge of this decision, but definitely leaning toward making the jump."

He took that in, and thought about it before responding. Al has always been good about thinking before speaking. He had one more question before actually sharing his thoughts.

"What will you do with your time? You should know the answer to this before making the jump."

"I thought long and hard about that, and I really don't think I'll be bored. First and foremost, my true friends are my neighbors, so I'll see you guys every day. Plus, Mark works irregular hours, so on those days when he's going to work late, we could probably get together for an hour or two. On top of that, I've been putting off home projects for a long time. As you know, there are always things to do in these old homes. This may surprise you, but I'd like to start reading more books. I like to read, but I never felt like I had the time or the energy for it when working all day."

This was enough information for Al. Something else he's always been good at is coming to rational conclusions after collecting key information.

"You should do it, John. Don't wait. You've clearly thought this through, and your reasoning is sound. I think you're ready for this, but I also think you're understandably nervous about it. It's a big step, but I'm telling you as a friend that you're ready."

"Hmmmm." That response was all I needed at that moment. He knew I was considering what he said, so he gave me more time. I was ready.

"You're right, Al. I'm going to give my notice to Con Ed when I get home."

But I gave it a second thought and remembered something I didn't consider before responding to Al's advice.

"No wait. I'll hold off until after Mark's big announcement that Isabel accepted his proposal. I want that to be his big moment, and I don't want to do anything that even comes close to stealing his thunder. I won't have to wait long though. Mark's chomping at the bit."

"You're a good friend, John. To all of us."

I gave him a punch in the arm. I don't know why I'm always surprised how solid his arms are when I do that. It reminded me how lucky Knife-Man was back in Daytona. He'll never know just how lucky he was.

"And you know what else, John?" Al's question was rhetorical.

"I'm going to start thinking more seriously about retiring as well. If my primary concern was possibly being bored, I think you just solved that for me."

This led to a conversation about the others. We agreed that Bruce would probably retire soon, especially since he's the oldest of the four of us. Mark, on the other hand, is the youngest. Additionally, we agreed that Mark's life is more closely tied to his business than the rest of us. For Mark, making and serving good food is his passion. Neither one of us thought he would even consider retiring for a long time, and possibly never.

It was about this time that the boat slowed to a crawl and there was an announcement that we were over the reef. Al and I made our way down to the lower level where the glass bottom provided a window to a whole new world.

The pink and white coral was the backdrop to an amazing kaleidoscope of colors, courtesy of beautiful fish of all varieties. To be honest, I really wasn't expecting much from this trip other than a nice relaxing boat ride, with some views of the islands. I seriously underestimated what I would see at the coral reef. There were probably thirty or more people gathered around the glass, but very few were saying a word. I guessed that most were just as surprised, and pleased by what they were seeing as I was. It was peaceful. It was spectacularly beautiful. It was a sacred moment.

Al summed it up perfectly with a single word.

"Wow."

We pulled back to the pier just a bit after 6PM. As we headed back to the hotel, we agreed there would be no sharing of our retirement conversation. That would wait until after Mark's engagement announcement, and after we had a chance to finally meet Isabel.

Mark and Bruce were sitting out in front of the rooms when we arrived, each drinking aggressive pours of what I guessed was Jameson whiskey.

"How was the game?"

"Bite me, Schumacher."

Al and I looked at each other and laughed. We both said the same thing at the exact same moment.

"They lost!"

We were still laughing when I walked over to Mark, scruffed up his hair, took his glass of whiskey, and helped myself to a swig.

"Don't worry, buddy, I won't say I told you so."

"I hate the Astros!"

"We all do Mark, we all do."

I went into the room, brought out the rest of the whiskey, and two more glasses. There was no more talk about the game, but we did suggest that Mark and Bruce take the boat ride before we leave Key West. They both indicated that they weren't interested. We tried. As agreed, Al and I were silent about retirement plans. We all just sipped the whiskey, and enjoyed the views from the pool. At that moment, nothing else in the world mattered. Well, that and our stomachs.

"Anybody up for Cuban Sandwiches for dinner tonight?"

Hands flew up enthusiastically in unison. Well, that was easy. I love unanimous votes!

14 – DAY NINE

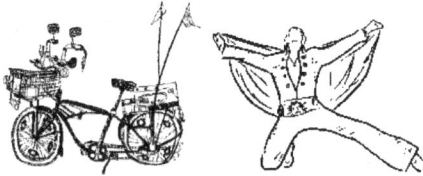

October 22nd

After having such a relaxing day, we all woke with the energy to work off some of the calories we'd been accumulating since we began this journey. We weren't under the illusion that anything we did today would even scratch the surface of what we would need to counteract the newly emerged pounds, but we figured that anything would be better than nothing. We skipped breakfast completely, unless coffee can be defined as breakfast. We could grab an early lunch (hopefully something like a nice healthy salad) after we got in our exercise.

The good news is that instead of jumping on a boring treadmill, here in Key West we could jump on bicycles and see more of the island. We had one day left on our bike rentals. The complete absence of hills would allow us to ride as long as we wanted without killing ourselves in the process. Mark, Bruce, and Al all wore their new Sloppy Joe's T-shirts. I mixed it up with my new Hogs Breath Saloon T-shirt. I momentarily considered telling

Mark that if this didn't scream, "Tourists," I don't know what did. But I refrained. Sometimes it's best to let sleeping dogs lie.

Al said he would take the lead on plotting the course with one of his iPhone apps, and setting the pace during the ride. He promised to take it easy on us. We filled our water bottles (again, not with water) and we were off.

We followed Al down Duval Street for a few blocks and turned onto Southard Street, which brought us onto the Truman Annex. This is the same route we took to go to the beach during the unexpected Key West D-Day Invasion. But prior to reaching the beach, Al had us turn onto Emma Street, taking us away from the beach and toward Mallory Square. The homes on this street were palatial. Protected by a combination of privacy walls, and palm trees, I could only imagine what the inside of these places must look like.

Before long, Emma Street changed its name to Front Street, where we passed what is called Truman's Little White House. This was President Truman's version of Kennedy's Hyannis Port, Nixon's Key Biscayne, and Bush's Kennebunkport. Just beyond this, the road forked. The main road went to the right. We veered slightly left, where we were met by a red brick walking path just prior to reaching Mallory Square. The walking area had some benches, so we stopped just long enough to take a quick drink of our liquid refreshments. We

176

were then instructed by Al, a bit too quickly, and a bit too loudly, to mount back up. We pushed on under the direction of our newly installed drill instructor.

"Do you have any idea where you're going, Al?"

Not that it mattered, but Bruce has never been comfortable when we start flying by the seat of our pants.

"Shut up, and keep up with me," was Alfred's only response.

It was clear to me, at least, that Al knew exactly where he was going. He intentionally chose a route that took us through neighborhoods that we never would have been able to appreciate if we were in the car. The neighborhoods that seldom saw tourists. It was quiet here... not at all like Duval Street... and the air had the sweet smell of hibiscus and gardenias rising from the gardens tucked safely behind the picket fences. Beyond these sanctuaries, the oceanfront reappeared. We followed Al past Higgs Beach, past Smathers Beach, and around Key West International Airport. We stopped for another refreshment break before making our way back on small side streets that lined the northern part of the island. Just before returning to the Historic District, we passed the Naval Air Station, Key West. I didn't even know a Naval Air Station existed on Key West until it was revealed to us via Al's route.

We all enjoyed the ride, but it was lucky we returned to familiar territory when we did. Even though the roads were flat, we all had reached our riding limits by the time we made it back to the bustle of Duval Street.

We decided to drop off our bikes at the rental shop a little early, rather than having to worry about it the next day. While there, we asked the owner for some ideas for activities that we may have missed along the way. Being a local, we figured he'd be more plugged in than we would ever be. He did mention a few possibilities that we had already done or just weren't interested in, and then added one that piqued our interest. He told us about a parade on Duval Street that evening that was part of the Fantasy Fest activities. He explained that the parade participants dress in wild outfits, some in nothing but body paint! He told us it would take place up around the Mallory Square end of Duval, starting around 7pm. It would end when it ended... no schedule existed for concluding the madness.

That gave us about an hour to go back to our rooms and freshen up before heading out again.

I knew this parade would be different than the ones we were used to on Staten Island, like the St. Patrick's Day Parade, and the Christmas Parade, and I really liked the idea of being out in the fresh air to watch all the craziness. With the sun down, the temperatures would drop into the low 70s making it very comfortable, and I also liked the idea that we would have the freedom to come and go as we pleased. Earlier, I was worried about not having any ideas for the day. I should have known Key West wouldn't let us down. I was now looking forward to seeing a new, and different type of parade with my friends. "New" and "Different." Exactly the point of this trip.

✳

There was no rest for the wicked. We went directly back to the hotel, took showers, changed our clothes, and ventured back to Duval Street. We didn't really know what to expect, and frankly it didn't really matter to us. We were just showing up with open minds, and ready to enjoy whatever it was this parade had in store for us. There were early signs of exactly what that would be. At least half the people we passed on the way had the most extravagant and outrageous costumes I'd ever seen. We saw Elvis, Freddie Mercury, Willie Nelson, Carmen Miranda, Jack Skellington, Edward Scissorhands, Ernest Hemingway (of course) and even Mozart! There was a sprinkling of vampires, zombies, and we saw a young lady up on the branch of a tree dressed as Spanish Moss.

Along the way, we found out that the parade was actually starting on Whitehead Street, but it would make its way up Front Street and then turn down Duval. By this time, the parade must have already started on Whitehead, assuming they started on-time, so we

decided to wait for it to come to us while we waited on
Duval, right where the parade would turn off of Front
Street. There was certainly no lack of entertaining sights
as we waited. By far, the most prolific sights were the
Drag Queens. They were all exquisitely dressed with
perfect make-up, and clearly having a great time while
basking in all of the attention.

While waiting for the parade to begin, Al made the
first sighting of body painting. I was looking down the
street, hoping to spot the first signs of the parade, when
Al nearly pushed me over.

"John, check this out. The cop!"

I looked where he was pointing, and there she was.
A young lady, very attractive, was dressed as a police
officer. But there was something different about her
uniform… everything above her waist was painted on.
No actual top, just paint! I must say though, if Al didn't
point her out, I don't think I would have even noticed.
The paint was that good. It was really amazing. Of
course, we alerted Mark and Bruce, and their stares were
far less subtle. I guess the whole idea of body paint is to
get people to stare, so… mission accomplished. As she
passed us, Mark put his arms straight out, as if inviting
her to put him in handcuffs. She just smiled and kept
walking.

"Easy, old man," Bruce said as Mark's arrest request
failed. "Remember, you're about to become betrothed!"

"Ha! You don't have to worry about me, my friend. I'm just enjoying the show."

There were many... MANY... more examples of body paint art. Most of them were easy on the eyes, but some were just PLEASE, NO. Regardless of who everyone was, or who they thought they were, or who they wanted to be someday, all were accepted, and all were having a good time.

I yelled out to my clan.

"I can see the front of the parade. They'll be making their turn in just a couple of minutes."

The parade was being led by a brightly colored musical band and dancers, followed by some floats. It was certainly an eclectic collection of floats and characters. Some of the floats included a pirate ship, a giant iguana, a Little Shop of Horrors float, and multiple floats that were sponsored by businesses around town, all decorated with brightly colored lights, and either attractive women, or men dressed as attractive women. There were dancers, singers, fairies or butterflies (I'm not sure which they were going for), guys in nothing but tutus, and dozens of golf carts creatively decorated.

It was one of the highlights of Key West for us. Certainly nothing at all like the parades we were used to on Staten Island. By the time 10pm rolled around, we were ready to sit down somewhere and relax.

Bruce had a good suggestion.

"We passed a Cuban coffee shop on the way here earlier. It has a sign out front saying they would be open until midnight. Probably because of the parade. Anyone up for a coffee?"

That was exactly what we wanted, and headed directly there. True to their word, the place was open, and was actually quite busy given that they were selling strong coffee so late at night. New York City calls itself the city that never sleeps. I have a feeling that there won't be much sleeping in Key West tonight either. We managed to get a table, and I went up to the bar to order four Cuban coffees and four scones. When I got back to the table, the others seemed to be in deep conversation. I immediately thought of an old Saturday Night Live skit.

"Hey, what is this? "Cawfee Tawk?"

I didn't have to explain the reference to my comrades.

"Well, it is now," said Mark. "Thanks for getting them. The scones look good."

"No problem."

"We were just talking about how fast time flies," said Alfred. "For instance, our parents have been dead for years, but for me, it seems like yesterday when they were with us."

Mark agreed, and added his thought.

"And going back even further than that, I remember the four of us as children… I mean real children, not just acting childishly… and in my mind it's like we just finished a game of street football, or shot some hoops up at P.S. 45."

"You're not kidding guys," I said. "I think about that kind of stuff all the time. I can go down the list – stickball, handball, flipping baseball cards, firecrackers in July, candied apples on Halloween. Where did those times go?"

Bruce laughed, and said he thought about those same things, and added a few of his own.

"And what about Barth's Corner Store where we would buy two-cent pieces of chocolate candy. If we had a quarter from our allowance, we could afford a Ring-Ding there!"

He had more.

"And remember walking by Mr. Decataldo's butcher shop? Sometimes, if he wasn't busy, he would stop us and give us a slice of fresh bologna, or one of those big pickles that he would wrap in wax paper."

"Yeah, I remember that Bruce," said Al. "He lived just a couple of houses down from us. He died before we finished high school."

We stopped for a minute. Partly because we wanted to taste the coffee and the scones, and partly because we needed to reflect on the implications of the conversation.

Alfred broke the silence.

"The bottom line is this. We are now in our mid-sixties and speeding towards a collision with the Grim Reaper. I don't feel old, but I'm not blind. I see how people call me sir, and how they open doors for me when they see me coming. I sold a car to a young lady a couple of weeks ago who told me I was adorable. Let me tell you something. If someone says you are adorable, you are either an infant or an old person... and I'm no infant."

We laughed, but it was a nervous and partially fabricated laughter. He was right, and we all knew it. I don't typically focus on the macabre, but since Al brought up the Reaper, I thought I'd take a pulse on the subject.

"Are you afraid of dying, Al?"

He seemed surprised by the question, but jumped right on his answer.

"You're damn right I'm afraid of dying. And I'm afraid of you dying, and I'm afraid of Bruce dying, and I'm afraid of Mark dying. What's not to be afraid of?"

No laughing this time. Just solemn nods. Mark responded to Alfred's question.

"I still feel like I've got a lot to do. Especially now that Isabel is in my life. I don't want to think about any of us not being here."

"I don't know if I'd say I'm afraid of dying," added Bruce "But I guess to some degree I am. I'm like you, Mark, in that I feel like there are still things I want to do before I go. Sometimes I feel old, and sometimes I feel irrelevant, but there are other times like right now on this trip, that I feel life still has a lot to offer. Do you know what I mean?"

I absolutely knew what he meant and I told him so. Another sip of coffee around the table, followed by samplings from the delicious scones. Weight control was not currently on our radar.

"Your turn, Schumacher. Are YOU afraid of death?" from Mark.

It was fair of the table to expect the dealer to play the card he dealt. I gave it my best shot.

"I used to be afraid of dying. I guess it was around the time I turned 50 that the fear started to peak. I began to have nightmares, and started losing sleep over the thought of it. But now that I'm older, I'm not really afraid of it anymore. I look at it now as a natural part of life, and I no longer try to make assumptions about what it means to die. What happens to us? Where do we go? That sort of thing. That just seems like a waste of time to me now."

I paused for a second to think about how to wrap up the thought. My friends instinctively understood this, and waited.

"Time flying by. That's what I'm afraid of. The older I get, the faster it flies. Everything I do... everything WE do... quickly becomes a memory. I know I need to live in the moment, to value each minute as it's happening. But in a flash, they're over, and I find myself reminiscing about them. Sometimes I find myself wishing I could slow down or stop time altogether, but I think the real solution would be to find a way to change my overall perspective. It's still our time to live. That's enough to keep my mind... our minds... busy. Our time to die isn't now, nor is it ours to worry about."

There was no immediate response. Some nods... but no comments at first. I wasn't really expecting one, but Mark finally offered his thought. I think he felt a need to lighten the mood.

"God damn, Shumacher! You almost put me to sleep."

I rewarded Mark's comment with a slap to the back of his head as I joined him, and the others in laughter. I told him to take another drink from his coffee so he could stay awake, and the conversation shifted to the Yankees loss to the Astros. I think Mark would have preferred a return to the subject of the Grim Reaper.

We refilled our coffees, and sat there in the coffee shop until they kicked us out at midnight. Another example of time flying... but I'm not going to reflect on that... I'll just try to enjoy the moment that life is now offering.

Hello reader! Did you miss me? I don't have anything

to add to the story, but I was wondering if you noticed that I haven't interrupted for a while. About a dozen pages or so. You are welcome!! OK... read on... read on...

We walked back to the motel. There were no signs that the partying in the streets had lost any of its energy, or had any likelihood of ending soon. That was fine with us, but we certainly had no intentions of adding fuel to that particular fire. We already had a full day, and I didn't need to take a vote to know that each of us was ready to hit the sack. We didn't have any set plans for the morning, but we would once again gather for breakfast somewhere and figure that out. My only plan at the moment was to put on whatever late-night show was currently on TV, knowing I would only last about ten minutes before yielding to a sound sleep.

*

Good, the guys are sleeping. Please excuse me for a minute dear reader. I need to talk with the other John for a minute.

Hey, John, since we are at a break point, I was wondering if this a good time to talk? I have a few questions I'd like to ask you if that's OK.

Sure. What's up?

I was just wondering, where you're going with this?

What do you mean?

Well, this story. Where are you going to take it from here?

Oh. OK. Well, I was going tell the readers more about the gang's time in Key West, prior to them heading back to Staten Island. They visit several more night spots such as the Green Parrot, and The Bull. I also thought it would be fun to talk about them hitting some of the touristy sites like the Hemingway House, and Southernmost Point. Maybe even tell them about the guys going on the Ghost tour that is offered on the island. Other than that, I wanted to hit on a few more of the Fantasy Fest events since the parade seems to have been such a success.

All of that sounds fine, but let me ask a harder question. Is this a story about things to do in Key West, or is this a story about the relationship between friends?

It's a story about friendship. It's also a story about how people of any age can grow, and expand their world-view, as long as they are willing to be open to new experiences.

Fantastic. That's what I thought. That being the case, I don't think you need to hit everything these guys did on their journey. We don't need or want to drive up the page count unless it's necessary to the core story you are trying to tell. The last thing you want is for it to come off sounding like a travelogue.

Hmmm. I see what you're saying. Do you think I've already over-stepped? Should I go back and delete some of the text about their experiences?

Well editing with a discerning eye is certainly important to any story, but no, I'm not concerned about what you have so far. Adding some local details, such as the history of Sloppy Joe's is fine as long as you think it would be of interest to the reader, and if it's not overdone. I would just recommend that you keep your eyes on the prize.

Got it! That's very helpful. Now that I think about it, none of those remaining activities that I just mentioned add to the message I'm trying to relay. The fun continues for the gang, but I think the reader already understands that this has been a special time for the guys. I don't need to pile-on with more examples of this.

That's honestly why I spoke up. I just wanted to make sure you understood the potential danger that any writer faces when writing a story. Don't stray from the message!

I think what I need to do at this point is to jump ahead to the gang's departure from Key West, and their drive home. This will help me stay on message, while streamlining the flow of the story for the reader. Thanks!

You are very welcome. I think you have a good path forward. Good luck with the rest of the story.

Thanks, man! I'll need all the luck I can get.

OK reader. Sorry for the interruption. Did you listen in on that conversation? If not, let me summarize. The other John is going to fast-forward to the gang's day of departure from Key West. I just didn't want you to feel like you've experienced "lost time." Believe me, there were no extra-terrestrials involved. Back to the story.

15 - DAY THIRTEEN

October 26th

We woke up with mixed emotions. This trip has been much more than any of us could have expected or hoped for, but we are also ready for the trip north. We've experienced the magical land of Oz, and everything it took to get there, but as Dorothy so correctly pointed out, there's no place like home.

The plan for today is to drive about twelve hours to Santee, South Carolina, spend the night there, then drive the final ten hours back to Staten Island. By 9am, the car was packed up, our coffee mugs and breakfast sandwiches from the 7-11 on Duval were in-hand, and we were rolling toward Stock Island and the rest of the Keys along the Overseas Highway. I volunteered to drive the first leg. Mark rode shotgun, while Al and Bruce were sound asleep in the back before we hit Islamorada.

"Hey, Mark, What's the first thing you're going to

do once we get back home?" I already knew what his answer would be.

"I'm going to go out to dinner with Isabel. I'll call her and set it up before we get home."

"Why don't you just call her now? Or text her?"

"Nah, I'd rather just keep it a private conversation. I don't need critics in the peanut gallery making stupid comments, and I'd rather talk with her than text her."

"Good choice. Definitely a Baby Boomer choice, but good none the less."

Mark looked to the back seat. He was checking to make sure the others were asleep. "I'll slip down to the lobby tonight after we arrive at the hotel and give her a call. She's a night owl and will still be up."

We sat quietly for a minute. I then told him what I think he already knew.

"Listen, Mark. I just want you to know that I'm really happy for you. I can't wait to meet Isabel, and I know we're all going to love her. She'll be lucky to have you."

"Thanks, John. I appreciate that." Then he added "Dork!"

I smiled, but had no words. I simply sent him a universal hand signal using a single finger. It's our way of putting a period at the end of a good conversation.

It was interesting to see our long trip in reverse order. When we reached Key Largo, I had to smile. It was a highlight for me, and the others, I'm sure. But we never slowed down or even considered one last peak at the Queen. Somehow, I felt that going back to try to relive our adventure would be anticlimactic. I believe the old saying is true; you can never go back. We need to keep moving forward toward whatever future we have waiting for us. I haven't started to seriously think about our next trip yet, but that will come in time. Until then, the four of us have built a huge cache of memories to sustain us.

Upon reaching the Florida mainland, and the Southern Glades, I kept a sharp eye out for prehistoric creatures, just in case Mark wanted to introduce himself to one of them again. None were spotted. I think the universe felt one encounter was enough. Florida fell one town at a time. Miami, Daytona, St. Augustine, and Jacksonville, all yielded to our northward trek. Georgia followed suit, disappearing in our rearview mirror. We made a quick stop just over the Georgia-South Carolina border to fill up on gas and grab some fast food. We made good time on this leg and pulled into Santee for our final overnight stop at around 9:30pm. There would be no adventures this night. We checked into the hotel, and all but one crashed immediately. Mark was the lone holdout. He had a phone call to make in the lobby.

16 – DAY FOURTEEN

October 27th – The Last Day of the Trip

Everyone must have been excited. By 7am, we were up, dressed, and in the café cramming down eggs, bacon, and muffins. We each grabbed a coffee to-go for the trip.

I pulled Mark aside.

"Did you get in touch with Isabel?"

"Yep, we're all set for dinner tomorrow night. I'm picking her up at 7pm and we're eating at LiGreci's Staaten."

"Wow, The Staaten. Fancy!"

"It has to be. I'm going to propose. I've decided to offer her my mother's ring, but if that's weird for her, we can pick a new one out together. Either way, I'll be happy."

I didn't say anything. I just hugged him. Surprisingly, he hugged me back without the hint of a snide remark.

Mark decided he would drive the last leg. He probably figured it would keep his mind occupied with something other than his upcoming proposal. At 7:45am, we were traveling north on Interstate 95 at eighty miles an hour. About an hour into the trip, Mark told Bruce and Al his plans for the following evening.

Alfred laughed, and patted Mark hard on his shoulder.

"Congratulations, man! You call me tomorrow after she says yes. I don't give a damn what time it is… you just call me.'

"Thanks, Al. Will do!"

Bruce was equally enthusiastic.

"Finally, one of us won't be a loser in love! Congratulations, Mark!"

Mark laughed. "Thanks, Bruce! But I don't think any of us are losers. We're old, we're obnoxious, we're impulsive… but losers? No way!"

As we made our way into North Carolina, I was reminded of the fact that we still had some unsmoked cigars.

"Any objections to cracking the windows and having a cigar?"

Al pointed out that this would be a good idea for more than one reason.

"Yeah, let's light one up for Mark. Afterall, once he's married, his cigar smoking days will be over."

Mark objected vigorously to this suggestion.

"Oh no! That's not going to happen. Besides dick-head, Isabel happens to like the smell of cigars. Her father used to smoke cigars, and the smell reminds her of him."

"Oh, is that what she told you?" countered Bruce. "We'll see when the time comes."

We fired up the cigars and leaned back in our seats as we watched the trucks and the pine trees pass by our windows. I put on a classic radio station (Mark's car didn't have Bluetooth), and we rocked out to Led Zeppelin and The Who until we lost the signal not far from the Virginia border.

We made another stop in Fredericksburg. This looked like another town that I'd like to visit someday, but today we just wanted to fill up the gas tank, and grab some grilled chicken sandwiches, fries, and milk shakes. Within 30 minutes we were back on the road. Anticipation was building. The next stop would be our homes on Staten Island.

The Washington DC beltway was a bitch... (We can't say we weren't warned) … but thankfully it kept moving. We passed through Baltimore without incident, and after that, the traffic thinned out considerably. I had to keep reminding Mark that we would get home faster if we weren't stopped by a cop for speeding. He tried, but the reminders continued from me for rest of the way to Staten Island.

We decided to take the Outerbridge Crossing onto Staten Island, rather than opting for the Goethals Bridge, which we took when we first left the island. As we made our way across the bridge, I felt a sense of calm come over me. This trip was my idea, and I felt a responsibility to ensure it went well. That responsibility has now been lifted. After two weeks, we were back on our home turf.

"Welcome to Staten Island, boys!" was the announcement from Mark.

The reaction was a combination of smiles, clapping, and WhooHoos. We took the West Shore Expressway to the Staten Island Expressway. We exited onto Clove Road, and took that to Bement Avenue. We turned right onto Morrison Avenue and made our final turn onto Davis Avenue at P.S. 45. We were home!

Mark pulled into his driveway and we all exited the car with some grunts, and a few limps for the first three or four steps.

Oh, you don't understand why? You must be a youngster. Wait till you're in your sixties.

We collected our bags from the trunk, turned towards each other, and stared in silence. We were thrilled to be home, and saddened that our epic trip was over. It was an odd moment. Alfred broke the deadlock.

"Well, guys... that's one for the record books. I'll never forget it."

He then held out his right hand, fingers together, palm down.

We all knew what that meant. It was one of our traditions. One that had been dormant for years. I put my hand on top of Al's... Mark placed his on top of mine... and Bruce placed his on top of Mark's. Our stacked hands started moving in a slow up and down motion like a piston.

Al then asked in a booming voice,

"WHO ARE WE?"

Our unified response was loud, and it gave me a chill as our hands flew apart into the air.

"WE ARE DAVIS AVENUE AND WE ARE ONE!"

✳

So, that's my story. I hope you liked it. I intended it to be an adventure undertaken by four friends who had lived their entire lives in one place, but who in their later years, decide to try something completely new. To travel to places they had never been before. It would become an adventure that changes the way these friends would view the world, and their places in that world. My hope was that you, the reader, would find it humorous and perhaps a bit insightful regarding the need for keeping an open mind, and an open heart regardless of one's age. I wanted everything to turn out for the best. A real "… and they all lived happily ever after" story.

But now… I'm starting to feel a push to tell you more. To tell you what I've been keeping from you… what I've been protecting you from. But I'm concerned it won't be what you want to hear. Life doesn't always play out the way we think it will, or the way we think it should. Sometimes our destiny… or should I say our fate… takes us down a different road.

So…Let's do it this way. Let me give you the choice of how this story ends.

If you are satisfied with the story as it currently stands – if you are content with how it has played out, and the way it concluded -- then great! Stop reading right here. You've more than earned the right to your satisfaction. If this is your choice, please allow me to thank you very much for sharing your precious time with me. Your kindness is more appreciated than you could ever know. Happy travels and Good bye!

John H. Steinmetz

The End

(Well... maybe)

17 – THE TRUTH

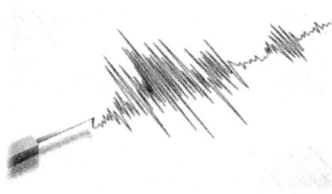

I see some of you are still reading. Just FYI... most people who see the words "The End," stop reading. OK, I guess you're curious (or maybe just gluttons for punishment).

It's certainly true that I intended this to be an adventure story involving four lifelong friends. Beyond that theme, however, is a story of regret. You see dear reader, much of what you just read is a lie. Not one designed to deceive, but rather an untruth created in my mind as a defense mechanism against a cruel reality. When you are left with nothing else, imagination can sometimes throw you a lifeline. It can help you create and live unrealized dreams.

The reality of this story is that the Davis Avenue Gang

never took that road trip to Key West.

I think it's best to rewind to an earlier part of the story and to allow the other John to take you to the finish line. What you are about to read would replace everything you read from the point where John was prepared to meet with the gang at O'Leary's Pub to see if he could get their buy-in to take the trip to Key West.

It was there, that a different decision was made. It was there that our two roads diverged.

When we met that night at O'Leary's Pub -- the night I proposed the trip -- things didn't go the way I had hoped; not by a longshot. Instead of everyone agreeing to the proposal, it was roundly rejected.

In retrospect, Mark, Bruce, and Alfred all had legitimate and reasonable objections to such an elaborate trip at that time. Bruce let us know that he had a doctor's appointment set for later in October and didn't think he could or should reschedule it. He didn't elaborate other than to indicate he hadn't been feeling well, and thought he should have it checked out. We didn't pry any further. If Bruce felt like he shouldn't put off a doctor appointment, none of us would have even thought to second guess that call.

Alfred said that there was no way he could afford to pause his dual-sources of income on such short notice, and suggested we shoot for a later date, giving him more time to prepare. This, of course, was not at all a surprise. I had assumed going in that if there was going to be an objection, it would most likely come from Al for exactly the reason he voiced. For the rest of us, our incomes would not have been impacted like it most certainly would for him. He relied on the commission from the car sales and his side gig as a freelance mechanic only generated income when he was there to work. There was nobody backing him up in either case.

The final nail in the coffin came when Mark told us for the first time that he was actually planning to buy-out Bennie's share of their jointly owned business. He said Bennie's father-in-law had been pushing him to sell his share of the restaurant and to come work for him in his growing restaurant supply business. It would mean more money, and much better hours for Bennie. From Mark's perspective, the buy-out would make him the sole proprietor of the restaurant. Something he had always hoped he would achieve. He would be standing on his own, able to make the changes he thought were needed to improve the business without negotiating with someone else. He said it would be several months before he would be able to break away. Completely understandable, and we were all excited for Mark about this big news.

So, my trip was put on the shelf for some later date. To be honest, I was kind of relieved by the outcome since I was a bit anxious about it myself. It would have been an intimidating trip for a group of guys so deeply planted in their hometown, and on such short notice to boot. When we left the pub that evening, we were all in good spirits and laughing it up. I had planted the idea of a trip in my friends' minds, and I was confident this idea would eventually grow to fruition. In the meantime, I would endure the occasional jabs from them about my crazy plan, while continuing to advocate for it until we could find a more convenient time for everyone.

A more convenient time. That phrase haunts me. You see, my friends and I will never make that trip to Key West. About a month after our gathering at O'Leary's, Mark was shot and killed. It happened on a Friday night, just a couple of hours after we broke up from our weekly sojourn to the pub. He told us when we first arrived that he had to make sure he was out by 9:30pm because Bennie, who was still co-owner of the restaurant with Mark for another month, needed to leave before 10pm. Even though it was Bennie's night to close, he asked if Mark would mind doing it. Bennie had last-minute plans to go away for the weekend with his wife. He told Mark he wanted to get a good night sleep before the trip. Mark agreed. So, when three men burst in to the restaurant with guns in hand, it was Mark who was there to face them. None of us, Alfred, Bruce, or myself, heard the shot from our homes, but we certainly heard all of the sirens. I looked from my bedroom window and saw police and fire emergency vehicles at the end of the street. All three of us converged nearly simultaneously at the side service entrance of the restaurant that faced our street. It was locked. As we rounded the corner to the front entrance, we were immediately met by police officers who were establishing a perimeter to keep everyone back. Our stomachs fell as we saw police marking off the entrance with yellow tape. Most of what happened, and what was said after that, is a blur. The only thing I remember clearly is the police officer telling us that Mark was dead; he knew Mark. The officer would stop in to the restaurant occasionally, and Mark would serve him free of charge. He said there was nobody else in the restaurant at the time. The three of us went silent. We couldn't say a word. My head was spinning, and I involuntarily went to one knee while I absorbed what we were told. We had just been with Mark that evening, and he wasn't even supposed to be working. I don't remember how I got home that night, or how I ended up in my living room recliner. I only remember waking up with the hope that it was just a nightmare. It was... but it also really happened. We later learned from police press releases that Mark apparently did not try to resist during the burglary, and he was found with his hands zip-tied behind his back with a bullet in the back of his head. The bastards could have just left with the money but instead, they killed him for no reason. To this day, nobody has been arrested for the murder.

After that, Al, Bruce, and I leaned on each other more than ever before. We met and talked daily just to reminisce, and to give each other an opportunity to vent if needed. It was often needed. We talked about our friendship, and our love for each other in ways that for men, only emerges after a tragedy... if ever. Even though our emotions were still raw, it was a time for healing. It didn't last.

Three months after Mark was killed -- barely enough time for us to even catch our collective breaths – Bruce died of a heart attack at work. I heard the news from a distraught Alfred. He had received a call from one of Bruce's coworkers who was also an acquaintance of Alfred. Al had apparently worked on the guy's car a couple of times after being recommended by Bruce. We learned that Bruce was in the middle of working on one of the offset presses and just dropped over dead. According to the coworker, he wasn't lifting anything heavy, and he seemed perfectly fine just minutes prior to collapsing. It happened that quickly. Bruce was always too heavy for his own good, and had some asthma issues that may have been related to his weight, but his death was completely unexpected, and totally devastating. Like Mark, Bruce died on a Friday.

Thinking back on it now, I wonder if this is why he was so hesitant to reschedule the doctor's appointment he mentioned that night at O'Leary's. I'll bet that's exactly why. Like the rest of us, Bruce never talked about whatever ailments he may have had, but he was also very responsible. I'm sure he would never have let a known medical issue go unchecked. I will miss all of his trivial facts about the city and his serious nature, even when surrounded by the adolescent foolishness that the rest of us constantly threw at him. His sudden end was shocking, but at least I know he didn't suffer. Sometimes you take consolation wherever it can be found.

And then there were two. Al and I shared our traumas as we had once shared our toys. Neither of us slept very well anymore, and our appetites for both food and life diminished. We started missing work days, something that would have been previously unconscionable. I forgave myself for all of this, recognizing that it was a natural reaction to loss. I encouraged Alfred to do the same. Life had changed for both of us, and it was never going to be the same, but we had to keep living. He recognized that as well and promised me he would be OK. After a couple of months though, Alfred wasn't rebounding. I started noticing something else. He was losing weight and complaining about abdominal pain. I started to worry that there might be something beyond mourning the loss of our friends going on with him. After pushing him for weeks, I finally got him to go to the doctor. The nightmare continued.

Just six months after Bruce's passing, Alfred died in his home under the care of hospice following his Pancreatic Cancer diagnosis. Did you guess it? Yes... he too died on a Friday. The day that I used to look forward to the most -- the day that the four of us met religiously for years -- has become my personal demon. The only saving grace in this part of the story is that Alfred and I had time to say goodbye. We knew what was coming, and we knew it wouldn't be long. I can't say that Alfred was my best friend. That would be like saying my favorite toe is the middle one on my left foot. I was lucky enough to have three best friends. I will say, however, that over the course of our lives I spent more time with Alfred than I did with Mark or Bruce. I think that's because of the four of us, he and I had the most in common. We had the same sense of humor. We were closest in age, and shared classes together when we were in school. As children, we both liked to entertain ourselves by building things like go-carts and tree forts with nothing more than whatever we could find laying around our houses. We also shared a relatively calm demeanor, especially when compared to Mark, who was high strung and occasionally volatile, and Bruce who was generally anxious and sometimes insecure person. Alfred and I even spent two weeks together as kids at a Lutheran summer camp. I could write a separate book just on that two-week experience. For now, I'll just say that our time there would later become the source of many hours of laughing and lighthearted disagreements as we each gave unique and conflicting versions of our camping exploits. Our last couple of days together on this planet were both heart-breaking and heart-warming. They were also very private. I will just say that Alfred stepped into the unknown with humor, bravery, and dignity. I will leave it at that.

So, within a year of shelving that trip to Key West, I lost all three of my travel companions and the three most important people in my life. The trip is no longer on the shelf. It died with my friends. I don't know what adventures we might have had, or what memories we might have made, and sometimes not knowing is the worst part.

Mark, Al, and Bruce were all cremated as requested in their wills. They are interred at St. Peter's Cemetery on Staten Island near Clove Lakes Park, where as kids we used to go sledding together in the winter. After Mark died, Alfred, Bruce, and I had the good foresight to buy the adjoining spaces at the cemetery next to our friend. We wanted to rejoin him, and each other, sometime in the future. None of us could have guessed that the future would arrive so quickly. My space is the last remaining vacancy.

If you're wondering about how I'm doing... well it seems I'm cursed with good health. My doctors tell me that my heart is as strong as an ox and based on testing, I run little to no risk of heart disease. My lungs are strong, and I can exercise longer and harder than the average man of my age. But most of all I'm lonely. Sometimes the loneliness is manageable, and at other times it's crushing. I miss my three friends, and I'm reminded of them every day I walk along Davis Avenue to and from the bus. I stare at my feet as I make that trek, avoiding the sight of three other houses that carry unbearable reminders.   All three houses were sold to young families with children. I should be happy when I see the children playing, but I feel the opposite. These are wonderful children, but when I see them playing on Davis Avenue, I'm reminded of my three lost friends. I wish I could be a better neighbor. I would like to bring their parents a welcome gift of some sort but I'm afraid they may invite me in to their houses, and I'm not ready for that. I will probably never be ready for that. I donated my Monopoly game to a church that has a youth program. It could never bring me the joy that it once had. I often find myself laughing about something one of them said or did over the years. The laughter, however, inevitably leads to a tear, which at my age is a little less taboo than it used to be. I remember hearing something several years ago that sticks with me today. It goes something like this… "When you are young, the world gives you things. When you are old, the world takes them away from you." And in the words of John Cougar Mellencamp, "Oh yeah, life goes on, long after the thrill of living is gone." Both of these are certainly true in my experience.

I was blessed to have Mark, Alfred, and Bruce as my friends, as my brothers, and I've been condemned to outlive all three.

This is my cross to bear. It seems that I was wrong all along. Living, not death, is my fate.

I'm back. Listen, don't blame me. I warned you! But let's be honest here. Doesn't this version of the story have a ring of truth to it? Assuming you're not very young, I'm guessing this version of events is relatable to you. Love, loss, loneliness… are these really foreign to anyone who has lived what we call a full life? I don't think so.

But don't worry. I'm not going to leave you here in this dark place. Something else happens that you need to know about. This road does not lead to a dead end of hopelessness. Read on.

18 – THE VISIT

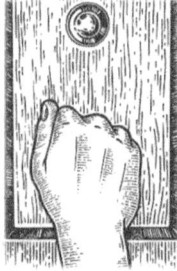

With my fate now fully revealed, what about my destiny? I always believed that the two were separate and distinct from each other. I also believed that my destiny was intertwined with those of Al, Mark, and Bruce. Was I wrong about all of that as well? For a while, after the death of my friends, I wondered if my worst fear had come true. That I had already realized my destiny, and I just didn't recognize it. Perhaps it was as simple as having the privilege of growing up with three amazing friends. That would certainly be something I could be proud of, but my mind was cloudy. It seemed like a question that I would never be able to answer to my complete satisfaction, so I put it out of my mind as best I could.

*

Then one day, there was a knock at my door. It was the first time anyone had knocked since the loss of my friends... my only visitors being the mailman, and the newspaper boy; neither having a need to knock. I almost ignored it completely, but I'm glad I didn't.

"Can I help you?"

"Good morning, sir! My name is Catherine Millings, and this is my friend Sasha Kobliska. Do we have the honor of addressing John Schumacher?"

"Well, I don't know how much of an honor it is, but yes, I am John Schumacher."

The two ladies almost seemed surprised, and then smiled widely.

"Wonderful! Would it be possible for us to come into your home so we could have a chat? We have an important message for you."

"Listen, ladies, I mean no disrespect, but I'm not interested in buying whatever you may be selling... nor am I interested in having my soul saved, if that is your intent."

Once again, the ladies flashed wide smiles, this time accompanied by a bit of audible laughter between them. The one who was doing all the talking so far, the one who said her name was Catherine, cleared her throat, and continued.

"Mr. Schumacher, I promise you that we're not here to sell you anything. As for your soul, it is not we who plan to do the saving. Please… give us ten minutes of your time, and if after that ten minutes you still want us to leave, we will abide by your wishes."

I started to reply. "Well…"

The older lady of the two, the one who hadn't said anything up until this point decided to interject with a strong accent.

"Please, it should be obvious that we are of no physical threat to you. We have come a long way to see you, and we wouldn't be here if it wasn't important."

I exhaled. I didn't have anything else going on, but inviting two strange ladies into my house clearly was nowhere on my agenda for the day. Never the less, I acquiesced.

"OK, come in. You have ten minutes."

They entered, mentioned something about me having a very nice house, and sat together on the couch in my living room. I offered them a glass of water, which they declined, and I sat down in the lounge chair across from them. I said nothing, only nodding as a signal that they could begin at any time. It was Catherine who spoke.

"We have a message for you from Mark, Bruce, and Alfred."

I stood up, surprised by how quickly my skepticism turned to anger.

"What is this? Who are you, and why are you really here?"

The one with the accent, Sasha, extended her hand with her palm outward, and quickly replied.

"This is a shock. Understandable. Please, we are not here to upset you."

"Well, I am upset, and I want some answers. You said earlier that you came a long way. Where did you come from?

"We drove here from Florida. A small town called Cassadaga. I'm sure you never heard of it."

When she mentioned Florida, I immediately thought of the aborted trip to Key West.

"That's correct, I've never heard of it, but what's your game? What do you want from me, and how do you know the names of my friends?"

Catherine took the baton from Sasha.

"Please have a seat, John. May I call you John? I think I should start from the beginning if that's OK with you."

My anger was replaced with curiosity, and I sat back down.

"Sure, you can call me John, and yes, start from the beginning."

∗

I had a feeling this wasn't going to be a ten-minute discussion, although I was reserving the right to call an end to it if need be.

Catherine leaned forward on the couch and began.

"First of all, John, please allow me to ask you two quick questions. Can I assume that your three friends, are fairly recently deceased?"

"Yes, that is correct."

"Allow me to speak for both myself and for Sasha when I tell you we are very sorry for your loss."

I was brief and to the point.

"Thank you. What is your second question?"

"While your friends were still alive, did the four of you make any plans for a trip? Perhaps to Florida?"

I was stunned and felt a cold chill run up my spine. I didn't answer immediately. I closed my eyes and took a deep breath. After a minute, I felt I could answer without my voice cracking.

"Yes. I had proposed a trip to Key West last October. For various reasons, we weren't able to pull it off, so we decided to wait. I was still hoping we could go at some point, and they seemed supportive of that, but they passed before we were able to go."

Catherine and Sasha made eye contact with each other, and nodded. Catherine asked Sasha if she wanted to say anything, but Sasha encouraged Catherine to continue.

216

"Thank you, John. I'm going to tell you some things now that will be hard for you to hear and hard for you to believe. That is perfectly normal. I just ask that you let us say what we came to say before showing us the door. Can you do that, John?"

"I think so. I guess it just depends on what it is you're dancing around."

She smiled.

"Well put! The first thing is a little about Sasha and myself. As I mentioned earlier, we are from Cassadaga, Florida. This is a town that is known to be the home of many psychic mediums. Both of us fit into that category of people who, for whatever reason, have special abilities."

I was wondering what I got myself into with these ladies, but decided to hear them out. She continued.

"Last week, both Sasha and myself were visited by your three friends. They made themselves know to us on the same night, but individually; me in my home and Sasha in hers. They came to us in dreams, in the form of three beams of light. They spoke, and their message to me was exactly the same message they gave to Sasha."

I held up my index finger, signaling the need for her to pause. She complied. I was trying to put all of this together in a way that would make sense.

"Why would my friends, if they wanted to send me a message, use two complete strangers to deliver this message? Why would they have not just given it to me directly?"

"They came to us because they knew of our abilities, and they knew you didn't share those abilities."

"But wait... they've never been to Florida and they never met you, so how could they have known about your abilities?"

"That is an excellent question, and your acceptance of my answer will almost certainly require you to take a leap of faith."

Catherine paused, and looked over to Sasha.

"Sasha, perhaps it would be best if you could step in for this part of the conversation."

Sasha nodded. "Of course."

Sasha made eye contact with me and tapped her lips a few times. I believe she was trying to decide the best way to explain the answer to my question.

"In our lives... in this dimension... time is linear. The seconds, minutes, hours, and days, all move in one direction along a rigid time-line. This is a law of physics that in our lives cannot be broken. Every day, we take actions based on decisions that we barely even think about, but those decisions, and associated actions drive our lives toward ends that we cannot alter."

Sasha paused. I think she was giving me an opportunity to ask a question, but hearing nothing from me, she continued.

"Your friends are no longer bound by our laws. They know about Catherine and myself because they can see what the future would have been if the decision to take that trip to Key West would have been different... if the four of you would have actually taken that trip. It would have been on that trip where we would have met all of you. Instead, you and your friends chose a different road to follow. The timeline that you are now living and everything that has followed, is based on that decision to stay home.

Silence. This was a lot.

Catherine broke that silence by thanking Sasha for her input. I kept quiet for a bit longer but Catherine and Sasha were patient. They waited. I was finally ready to push ahead.

"OK, I'm going to take the leap here and assume that this is all legitimate, and that my friends are trying to get a message to me through the two of you. So go ahead, what is the message?"

Sasha responded this time.

"First things first. Would you mind sitting silently for a couple of minutes? Please indulge us one last time."

"Uhhh... OK... why not."

I sat silently as Sasha and Catherine dropped their heads for a minute or so. When they raised their heads, they stared at something that was not visible to me.

"Do you see it, Catherine?"

"I sure do!"

They closed their eyes and dropped their heads again for another minute.

"We're now ready to give you their message, John," said Catherine. "We ourselves did not know what the message was until just this minute. In Florida, we were only given your name, your address, and instructions to read your aura. Do you know what an aura is, John?"

"Not really. I've heard of them. I seem to recall reading that they surround people... and something about different colors."

Catherine gave a facial expression that made me think she liked my answer. She then nodded in agreement and continued.

"We don't need to get into great detail about auras. Your rudimentary understanding is a good start. I'll just add that auras are an energy field, or a luminous body that surrounds your physical body, and the different colors within a person's aura represent different aspects of that person's human characteristics."

Sasha then jumped in.

"Yes, and we had no idea why we were asked to read your aura by your friends, but it became pretty clear when we did so. Your friends are very clever!"

"Yes, I know they're clever, but are you telling me you drove all the way from Florida to deliver a message you didn't even have?"

"Well... we had enough information to know we had to make the trip," Sasha said.

"Indeed," replied Catherine, "and we've learned to trust our feelings when it comes to communicating with the other side. We had faith that the message would be revealed to us at the correct time. It has done just that."

"OK" I said. "I'm ready to hear it if you are ready to tell it."

"Sasha, would you like to tell him?" Catherine asked.

"No, my dear. You can tell him."

Catherine walked over to me and looked me in the eyes. She put her hand on my shoulder and she said something that I wasn't expecting. I don't really know what message I was expecting to hear. Perhaps that my friends loved me, or that they would wait for me wherever they are. But that wasn't the message.

"They want you to know that they never left you. That they are with you right at this moment... beside you... and they would walk with you on the rest of your life journey. And when that journey is complete, the four of you would march together again."

Catherine paused for a second. She seemed to remember one more important point.

"When Sasha and I read your aura just a moment ago, we saw that you were surrounded by three beams of light. The same lights that we saw when your friends visited us in Florida."

I sat down. I had to. I didn't know what to say, and I didn't know what to think. My emotions, like my head, were spinning, and I felt my eyes welling up with tears. But I didn't know if they were tears of happiness or sadness. When I woke up that morning, the day held no promise for me. My plan was the same plan I've had for months – to just get by. Now I was facing the prospects of something that was exciting, but also terrifying. Should I or should I not, allow myself to believe all of this? I felt like I needed to hear everything Catherine and Sasha had said since entering my home one more time. Maybe, I would be able to make sense of this if I had another shot at it. As it was, I didn't know what to believe. But at that moment, I knew what I WANTED to believe. I wanted to believe that what these ladies were telling me was true. If that were the case, it would mean that my friends had not dissolved into some black hole of nothingness. It would mean that they continue to exist, and even though I may not understand their new existence, I would be thrilled to be able to stop worrying about their darkness as well as my own. And the best thing is – they are trying to reach out to me, letting me know they are still with me. If I believe this and it turns out to be some kind of scam or fraud, I don't think I would be able to recover from it. I wasn't sure if I wanted to be that vulnerable with what I had heard so far.

I reengaged.

"Ladies, as you have obviously expected, everything you told me so far is mind blowing, and hard for me to accept. I have no idea what you would have to gain by driving here from Florida, just to tell me a lie, especially since you are not asking for any money for your services. My heart wants to believe what you are telling me, but my brain is warning me to be cautious. You know my name, you know my address, you know the names of my friends, and that they have died, but all of that can be found fairly easily on the internet. I think this is something I'm going to have to give a lot of thought, and probably a prayer or two."

Catherine smiled again. I liked that she was so quick with a smile.

"Well, John, apparently your friends know you very well. They anticipated your very understandable skepticism, and other than your name and address, they also provided us with something that we could not otherwise know. It is something that neither Sasha nor myself understand, but that makes sense given its purpose. I would like to share it with you, and I hope it will be helpful for you.

"OK," I said. "What is it?"

"They told us to simply say "No Chips.""

I lost my breath. My friends just BROKE what I thought I knew about my life, and they wanted me to know that there would be <u>no payment due</u> from them. There was now no doubt in my mind about what I was told by Catherine and Sasha was absolutely true. They had presented me with a gift that I could never repay, even if they were willing to accept some form of compensations, which they were not. I didn't actually respond to the "No Chips" comment. It wasn't necessary. I don't think either lady needed to be psychic to know it had made all the difference. When I was able to refocus my eyes through the tears, I saw them both sitting on the couch smiling.

"What can I do to repay this blessing. Ask me for anything, and if it is mine to give, it will be yours."

Both continued to stare and smile. I'm not sure, but I thought I detected that they too were fighting back some tears. Sasha responded to my offer.

"You have already repaid us in full, John. You allowed us into your home, even though we were complete strangers, and you listened to us when we asked you to give us a chance to explain our visit. Thanks to you, we were able to keep our promise to your friends. Their message has been delivered. I hope you know, and appreciate, how lucky you are to have such good friends."

"I did. I mean, I do."

"If the offer is still good, we will take those glasses of water now." said Catherine.

I laughed, and they joined me in kind.

The ladies spent most of the day with me. I shared stories with them about Al, Mark, and Bruce. We laughed, and I think they blushed upon hearing a couple of the stories. I hadn't laughed like that in a long time. It was freeing. They didn't plan to leave until the next day, and told me they had a room at the Holiday Inn on the south side of the island. I told them they should cancel their reservation, and spend the night in my empty bedrooms. They thanked me for the offer but graciously declined. Their room payment was non-refundable, and the hotel also offered them easy access to the highway for their long trip back to Florida the next morning. I asked them for their addresses and phone numbers, which they happily provided. I don't know if I'll ever make it to Florida, but if I do, they will be my first stop. If not, they will at least receive a Christmas card from me every year.

$$*$$

I no longer live my life one day at a time, and one foot in front of the other. I have regained the ability to look to my future with hope and optimism. I still miss my friends, of course, but knowing that they are with me, even if I can't see them, gives me energy.

Regarding my destiny, I now know that it has not passed me by. Thanks to the message delivered by Catherine and Sasha, I am living my destiny every moment of every day that I am alive. I am destined to be a good neighbor, a good co-worker, and a good-friend. The best part about the work of fulfilling my destiny is the knowledge that I won't be alone. I'll always have the love and support from three angels to help me whenever I need it. What more could I ask for?

19 – GENERATIONS

I made three chicken casseroles the other day, and delivered them to my new neighbors who now occupy Mark's, Al's, and Bruce's old homes. It was strange to be back in the houses, but it was also good. These old houses were now homes for a new generation who have revitalized them. New carpets, fresh paint, new love, new life. I thought to myself that my old friends would have liked my new friends very much, and they would have been pleased that these were the families now occupying their homes. The young couples asked about the previous owners. I had plenty to tell them. Much more than they expected to hear from me I presumed, but they appeared to be completely engrossed in my stories of the past, and encouraged me to continue when I suggested I was probably boring them. They laughed with me, and I think perhaps I even detected some tears when I mentioned how much I missed Al, Mark, and Bruce. I apologized for that but they quickly reassured me that it was OK and thanked me for my candor. They told me how happy they were to hear that their new homes held so many treasured memories.

I brought each of their children a toy. I was definitely out of my depth in the toy store shopping for age-appropriate gifts. I had no idea what kind of toys kids liked at their various ages, but I was assisted by an employee who was very helpful, and who apparently nailed it with her suggestions. I had forgotten how loud children can screech with glee when opening presents. By the time I left, I was exhausted just watching them play! Everyone was wonderful, and I hope to stay in touch with them, both parents and children, as often as possible. I may even buy another Monopoly game, and teach the kids how to play when they are a little older. I'll make sure the house rules are less ruthless until they are MUCH older. Staten Island has always been a good place for families, especially on Davis Avenue.

I've learned to love life again. I don't know how much time has been allotted to me in this life, but I do know that I have nothing to fear. I know that someday there will be a grand reunion between four friends. And what a reunion that will be! That makes me smile.

***

One final thought. I recently heard someone famous... who for the purposes of this story will remain nameless... describe what he thought was the difference between happiness and joy. He said that happiness is something that is given to you by someone else. You are given a present, or you are given a compliment, or you are given a promotion. These things make you happy. But that happiness is fleeting, and it's dependent on others. Joy, however, is different. Joy is something you carry in your heart. Nobody can give it to you, and nobody can take it away from you.

I think this is a universal truth. Happiness is great, but it won't get you through those inevitable tough times in your life. That's where joy comes in. You will still experience those tough times – loss, loneliness, fear, anger and so on. Those emotions are part of life. Your only shield is a joyous heart.

So, for those of you who went on this journey with me, I wish you all joyous hearts, and a lifetime of close friendships.

Good bye, Friends. Thank you for sticking with <u>BOTH</u> of us!

John "NARRATING" the story
&
John "TELLING" the story

The End

(Really!! Go take a nap!!)

ACKNOWLEDGMENTS

Grateful acknowledgement is made to the following for their support and encouragement to this book.

Melanie Steinmetz – My wife encouraged me throughout the entire process and she provided the first level of editing and feedback, which were critical inputs when I needed them the most.

Jackson & Ellen Copley – Jackson is an extremely talented author who provided me with guidance and valuable inputs to this book. Ellen, Jackson's wife, lent me her keen talent for editing as well as her encouragement. Jackson and Ellen are co-owners of Contour Press, the publishers of this book.

My sons, Daniel & Michael, and their wives, Stephanie & Melissa – Among the first readers of the earlier drafts, my family was very kind regarding their feedback of this story.

Cathy Steinmetz – My sister Cathy is a special person and her feedback was equally special. Thanks Sis!

Mary Holland – Mary is a friend whose background as a producer gives her a special insight into story telling. She took the time to read and edit my book.

Kathy Cartagena – Kathy is an evidential medium who conducts readings and seances in Cassadaga, Florida. Kathy read my book and validated parts that were relevant to her field of expertise.

Claudia Sperl – Claudia did a magnificent job with the cover art for this book. I can't thank you enough Claudia!

Made in the USA
Middletown, DE
21 May 2023